Skamble Skimble

Fairy tales

Skamble Skimble

Fairy tales

ISBN/EAN: 9783337024390

Printed in Europe, USA, Canada, Australia, Japan

Cover: Foto ©Andreas Hilbeck / pixelio.de

More available books at **www.hansebooks.com**

FAIRY TALES,

BY

SKIMBLE SKAMBLE.

Sometimes he angers me
With telling me of the moldwarp and the ant,
Of the dreamer Merlin and his prophecies,
And of a dragon and a finless fish,
A clip-winged griffin and a moulten raven,
A couching lion and a ramping cat,
And such a deal of skimble skamble stuff
As puts me from my faith.
SHAKSPEARE, HENRY IV, PART I.

DURHAM:
ANDREWS & Co.
LONDON:
WHITTAKER & Co., PATERNOSTER ROW.
1869.

DEDICATION.

To all merry, good-tempered, and well-behaved, children, who are, of course, fond of Fairy Tales, and to all grown-up people who are not stiff and starched, but are fond of children, and buy them books on their birthdays and at Christmas, these Tales are dedicated, with much affection, by their friend,

SKIMBLE SKAMBLE.

CONTENTS.

THE DARK WOOD.

RINCE Chang-quee, the son of the
Emperor of China, was once on a visit
to King Khosroes, who was the King
of Persia. The King of Persia had a
daughter, the Princess Fairhairina, whose hair
glittered like gold, and whose skin was as white
as milk. Both the Prince and Princess were very
young, and they used to play together. The
Princess's governess, the Lady Straightlace, used
to tell her she must never play with the Prince
in the sunshine, lest she should get sunburnt.

"My dear," she said, "I had rather you never
went out at all except in the close carriage; it is
of such importance that you should keep your
milk-white complexion; but, as you are so fond
of playing with the Prince, you may go with him
out of doors when the sun is not shining: even
then you must take care to keep under the trees,
and have your sun-bonnet and large parasol."

Princess Fairhairina did not like this, it was so pleasant to be out in the sunshine, and it was such a bother to be always carrying her parasol. So she used to slip away with Chang-quee when the Lady Straightlace was not looking, to a large breezy open moor not far from the palace, and there she threw her sun-bonnet and her parasol on the ground, and romped about in the sunshine to her heart's content. And, for all that, her skin kept as white as ever, and the Lady Straightlace never found it out; which shows how foolish it was of her to be so very particular. This moor was covered with heather, which was all purple when it was in blossom, and smelt delightfully; and thousands of bees used to be humming among it, and gathering honey. But they never stung the Prince and Princess, who took care never to hurt them, and were not afraid of them. On the further edge of the moor there was a large dark wood, into which the Prince and Princess never ventured to go, it looked so gloomy. Sometimes, when they lay on the heather, looking fearfully into the wood, they fancied they saw strange figures moving about under the dark shadow of the pine-trees ; little wee men grinning and playing antics; or creatures with bodies like men and faces like dogs or monkeys. Once or twice Fairhairina thought

she spied a stately figure with a red mantle and
a golden crown; and Chang-quee thought he
saw a lady with a long green train and diamonds
in her hair. But, if they saw these things at all,
it was but for a moment, for they seemed to
vanish directly. So they said to each other it
must be fancy; and the heather, and the bees,
and the sunshine, and the breeze on the moor,
were so pleasant that they soon forgot their fears,
and played about till it was time to go home.
Still they could not help thinking there was something strange about that dark wood, and they
often dreamt about it.

One day, as it was growing late, they saw a
beautiful white hare running towards the wood
across the moor, with a great ugly black dog
after it. So Chang-quee, who was a brave little
prince, and kind to any creature that seemed in
trouble, ran after the dog and threw a big stone
at him; and the hare escaped into the wood, but
the dog seemed to vanish. Another day there
was a beautiful white dove flying towards the
wood, and a great black hawk after it; and
Chang-quee took his bow and arrow and shot at
the hawk, and the dove got safely into the wood,
but they saw the black hawk no more. Another
day there was a beautiful little white mouse running hard towards the wood, and a huge ugly

snake wriggling after it, with it's great mouth
open. So Chang-quee ran after the snake with a
stick and hit it on the head, and the mouse got
into the wood, but the snake vanished. These
things made them think all the more that there
was something strange about that dark wood.
But still they came and played on the moor
whenever the Princess could get away from the
Lady Straightlace, for they were brave young
folks, and, as they never did any harm to anything, they were not afraid.

Now, one day, when they were playing on the
moor, they could not help feeling sad; for Chang-
quee had stayed with the King of Persia just seven
weeks, and was to go back to China next day.
This was enough to make them sad, for they
could not help thinking how happy they had been
on that sunshiny moor, and that this would be the
last time they could play there together. So they
sat together looking into the wood very sad indeed; so sad that they could not help feeling as
if some great misfortune were going to happen.
All at once Fairhairina said, " Look, Chang-
quee! there's that stately figure with the red
mantle and the golden crown, and he seems to be
beckoning to me to come to him." But Chang-
quee could see nothing; nor could Fairhairina
after she had spoken. Soon she said, " I must

just go to peep into the wood, and try if I can see him again." Chang-quee tried to dissuade her; but she said she must go: so she tripped away to the edge of the wood and peeped under the dark pine-trees; and then a shadow seemed to hide her from Chang-quee, and he could see her no more. So he ran down into the wood after her, and called her name over and over again, but there was no answer but the echoes of his own voice, which seemed as if they would never stop, and nothing to be seen but dark shadows of trees, which seemed as if they had no end. So Chang-quee came out of the wood again, thinking that she might have come out too, and that he should find her on the moor; but he found nothing there but her sun-bonnet and parasol, which she had thrown down upon the heather. Oh! how miserable he was when he saw these, and thought that his little Princess who had worn them was gone! But there was nothing to be done but to take them up and return home.

The King, as you may suppose, was in a terrible way when he heard about it. He at once ordered the Lady Straightlace to be thrown into prison for not taking better care of the Princess. And he sent explorers into the dark wood; but they could not find her. So he despatched mes-

sengers all over the world, to proclaim that who-
ever could find the Princess should marry her,
and be King after his own death; and he de-
clared that, if she was not found within a year,
both the Lady Straightlace, and all the ladies
who attended the Princess, and all the nobles of
his court, should be put to death. And he sent
word to the Emperor of China that he would
keep the Prince Chang-quee fastened up in a
golden cage till the Princess was found. So
Chang-quee was put into a golden cage, and fed
through the wires like a bird; and he did nothing but mourn day and night for his lost companion. Now, when the Emperor of China heard
that his son was fastened up in a golden cage by
the King of Persia, he was very angry; and he
sent word that, if he was not sent home to China
safe and sound within a year, he would invade
Persia with a great army. But the King of
Persia did not care for this, and kept him still in
the golden cage. At length, when the year was
nearly over, Chang-quee asked the nobleman
who fed him through the bars of the cage to beg
the King to come and speak to him; and the
King came, and Chang-quee said to him,—

"Mighty King, the year is now nearly over,
and, if you do not relent of what you have said,
a number of innocent people will soon be put to

death, and that will not help to find the Princess ; and my father will be here with his great army, and will waste your country with fire and sword ; and that will not help to find the Princess. Put off your purpose for another year, and let me out of this golden cage, that I may go through the wide world to find the Princess. And, when my father hears that I am free, he will lead his army home again, and perhaps I may succeed in finding the Princess after all, and that will be much better for everybody than cutting off so many heads."

And the King thought a bit, and then said that Chang-quee had given good advice, and it should be as he had said. So he was let out of the golden cage, and set out through the wide world to try to find the Princess.

First, he went to the South wind ; but the South wind had not seen her. Then he went to the East wind ; but the East wind had not seen her. Then he went to the West wind ; but the West wind had not seen her. The way to the North wind was through the great dark wood ; and those whom the King had sent there to explore told him that it was impossible for anyone to find his way through it, and that there was nothing in it but darkness and wild beasts. Chang-quee would have gone there first of all if

they had not dissuaded him, but now he said he
would go, and nobody should stop him. So he
took a strong stick in his hand, and slung his
bow and arrows over his shoulder, and hung a
bag over his back having in it six loaves of
bread and three bottles of wine, and went into
the great dark wood. For three days he went
on, and it got darker and darker, and at night he
heard growls like the voices of wild beasts; but
no living creature did he see.

On the evening of the third day he met a little
man with a red jacket and a white feather in his
cap, who said to him, " How now, Prince
Chang-quee, whither wanderest thou ?"

And the Prince replied, " I am in search of
the North wind to hear tidings of the Princess
Fairhairina, who was lost a year ago. But how
is it that you know my name?"

And the little man answered, " Do you remember one evening killing a snake that was
pursuing a white mouse on the moor? I was
that little white mouse, for I change myself into
a white mouse when I go out on the moor, and I
have not forgotten your kindness. Go on for nine
days more, and you will meet the North wind,
and he will tell you where the Princess is. But
take this cloak ; you will want it when the North
wind breathes upon you." With that the little

man gave him a woollen cloak wrapped up in a nutshell.

"Thank you," said the Prince; "but pray what is your name?"

"My name," said the little man, "is Jerry-banoo."

Then the Prince journeyed on for three days more; and on the evening of the third day he met a very little lady, who danced as she walked, and never kept still.

"How now," said she, "Prince Chang-quee, "whither wanderest thou?"

And he replied, "I am in search of the North wind to hear tidings of the Princess Fairhairina, who was lost a year ago. But how is it that you know my name?"

And the little lady answered, "Do you remember one evening killing a black dog that was pursuing a white hare across the moor? I was that white hare, for I change myself into a hare when I go out of the wood, and I have not forgotten your kindness. Go on for six days more, and you will meet the North wind, and he will tell you where the Princess is. But take these shoes; you will want them when the time comes."

"Thank you," said the Prince; "but pray what is your name?"

"My name," said she, "is Jiggerina."

Then the Prince journeyed on for three days more, and on the evening of the third day he met a beautiful lady with a green train and diamonds in her hair, who said to him, " How, now, Prince Chang-quee, whither wanderest thou ?"

" I am in search," said he, " of the North wind, to hear tidings of the Princess Fairhairina, who was lost a year ago ; but how is it that you know my name ?"

" Do you remember," she replied, " killing a black hawk that was pursuing a white dove across the moor ? I was that white dove, for I change myself into a dove when I go out of the wood, and I have not forgotten your kindness. Go on for three days more and you will meet the North wind, and he will tell you where the Princess is. But take this diamond, and rub it when you are in your greatest distress, and I will come to help you."

" Thank you," said the Prince ; " but pray what is your name ?"

" I am," said she, " the Queen of all the Fairies."

Then the Prince journeyed on for three days more ; and on the evening of the third day he felt a cold, cold wind meeting him through the wood, and he knew it was the North wind coming. And it was so cold, so cold, so very cold, that he thought he should have died. But he bethought him of the cloak that the little man had given him, and took it out of the nut-shell and put it on, and then he could meet the North wind. And the North wind told him that he knew where the Princess was, and would carry him to her. So he got on the North wind's back, and went sweeping through the air he knew not whither. At last the North wind put him down, and told him that the Princess had been carried off by the Fairy King of the Burning Mountain, and that his palace was yonder, where a light appeared in the distance. The North wind said he could not go there himself, as the heat of the Burning Mountain would be the death of him, but Chang-quee might go and try his luck. So Chang-quee went on towards the light; but by-and-by such hot sparks came flying through the air from the Burning Mountain, and the stones 'under his feet grew so hot, that he thought he should have died. His hair was scorched, and his shoes were burnt off his feet. Then he bethought him of the shoes that the little lady had given him, and he put them on. And all at once he found he could run like the wind across the hot stones without feeling them; and he ran so fast that the sparks had no time to scorch him, and he soon came to the palace of the Fairy King of the Burning

Mountain. It glittered like the sun with gold and precious stones, and, as the great gates were open, he went fearlessly in. And he wandered through innumerable halls so bright with jewels that he could hardly see, till at last he came to a room at the top of the palace, where he saw his Fairhairina sitting on a throne with her hair like gold, and her skin like milk, and surrounded by a guard of fairies with eyes like fire; but he rushed through them all, and clasped the Princess in his arms. And she told him that the Fairy King of the Burning Mountain kept her there because she would not marry him, but that she was treated with great respect, and all the fiery-eyed fairies had orders to obey her in everything; but that she could not escape from the palace because of the hot stones that surrounded it, and the sparks from the Burning Mountain.

Then the Prince requested her to send the guard of fairies away; and, when she had done so, he told her that he had a pair of shoes that would enable them to run over the burning stones like the wind, and that she should put one of them on and he the other, and they would try and escape together. So the Princess was very glad, and said she would try, but there was no time to be lost, as the Fairy King of the Burning Mountain, who had gone off on a hunting excur-

sion, would be back next day. Then she rose
from the throne and went with Chang-quee
through the palace, and none of the fairies ventured to stop them, as the King had given them
orders to obey Fairhairina; and when they got
outside, they each put on one of the magic shoes.
But they could not go nearly so fast as Chang-
quee had done, because they had only one shoe
a piece; and before they were half way across the
burning stones, the Fairy King of the Burning
Mountain, whom one of the fairies with fiery eyes
had told of their escape, overtook them. He was
in his red mantle, and wore his golden crown,
and he looked as stately as ever, and very angry.
Anger flashed out of his fiery eyes as he ordered
his attendants to take Chang-quee and throw him
into the fiery hole at the top of the Burning
Mountain, and to conduct the Princess back to the
palace, but to treat her still with all respect, for
he loved her very much, and hoped still to persuade her to be his wife.

Then Chang-quee bethought him of the diamond which the Fairy Queen had given him, and
he rubbed it; and all at once she appeared before
them. And she spoke to the Fairy King of the
Burning Mountain, and said, " Proud King,
wherefore dost thou detain this fair maiden

against her will, and threaten death to this brave
youth, who is worthier of her than thou ? Know
that I have taken them under my special protection, for they once did me a good turn when I
happened to be abroad in the world and unable
to protect myself. I command thee therefore to
set them free, or I will wave my sceptre three
times in the air, and thy palace will crumble into
dust, and thou wilt become a heap of ashes."

Then the Fairy King of the Burning Mountain, who knew that the Queen of all the Fairies
was more powerful than he, bowed before her,
and submitted to her will. And the Queen of all
the Fairies placed Chang-quee and Fairhairina
in one of her state carriages drawn by twelve
white doves, who flew with them through the
air, and set them down on the sunny breezy
moor just outside the dark wood, where they had
so often played together.

O, how glad they were to be once more there,
and out of all their dangers! And, when they
got to the King of Persia's palace, what rejoicings
there were! The Lady Straightlace was brought
out of her prison, looking very thin from her
long confinement; and the Emperor of China,
Chang-quee's father, who had just arrived with a
great army to take vengeance on the King of

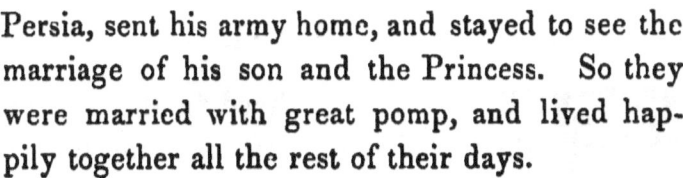

Persia, sent his army home, and stayed to see the marriage of his son and the Princess. So they were married with great pomp, and lived happily together all the rest of their days.

THE ELF IN THE RABBIT WARREN.

CHAPTER I.

THE old crow that lived in the nest on the top of the fir tree near the King's palace was talking to his wife, and said, "Have you seen the poor little elf to-day that lives in the rabbit warren on the top of the hill?"

"No," said the old crow's wife, "but I am often sorry for him, for he must be very lonely. Do you know why he lives there all by himself, and what is his name?"

The old crow gave her no answer but Crr, crr, crr; which meant, in the crow's language, "I know a good deal, but I shan't tell *you*, old woman." For the old crow was a crusty old crow, and did not choose to tell his wife every-thing. So they sat at the top of the fir tree with-out speaking for some time. At last the old crow said, "Do you think we could get him a wife? He would be much happier with one, than living, as he does, all alone with the rabbits. I would tell you something about him if you could manage that, old woman."

" There's nobody I can think of," said the crow's wife, " so likely as the King's little daughter, Skip-and-jump ; but it would be hard work to get her, for her nurse, Snick-snack-snorum, is always with her, and keeps such a sharp eye upon her. How do you think we can manage it ?"

To this the old crow only said, Crr, crr, crr. And they sat again for a long time, and said nothing. At last the old crow said, " If anybody can help us it will be the jackdaw." So the old crow's wife flew away to fetch the jackdaw.

The jackdaw lived in the yard of the King's palace, and had one wing cut off to prevent his flying away; and the King's little daughter, Skip-and-jump, often played with him. So the crow's wife found him in the yard, standing on one leg on the edge of the trough, and winking with one eye, and asked him to come up the fir tree and have a chat with her and her old man. And the jackdaw went, for he was fond of a bit of gossip. But he had hard work to get to the top, because of his wing being cut off. But the crow's wife helped him up, and he reached the top at last.

" Well," said the old crow, " how do you do,

Jack? I and my old woman have been talking about the poor little elf that lives in the rabbit warren at the top of the hill, and pitying him for being so lonely. Do you think you could persuade the King's little daughter, Skip-and-jump, to go and see him? We think she would be a nice companion for him."

"I don't know how that may be," said the jackdaw; "her nurse, Snick-snack-snorum, keeps her so tight, and is so very particular: but I'm a sly bird, and I don't mind trying. But can you tell me why the little elf lives there all by himself, and what is his name?"

To this the old crow only said, Crı, crr, crr. So the jackdaw saw it was no use asking him, and talked about other things. And they had a nice little lunch of delicious wriggling little worms, which the crow's wife brought for them, and then a dessert of wheat fresh out of a newly-sown field. And, after enjoying himself very much, the jackdaw hobbled down again, and went and sat on one leg, winking with one eye, on the edge of the trough, in the King's yard, thinking all the time as hard as he could, till the King's little daughter should come out. By-and-bye she came, when she had done her lessons, with her nurse Snick-snack-snorum.

Skip-and-jump was a very nice little girl,

dressed as a King's daughter should be, in a beautiful little frock made of silk and gold which glittered in the sunshine. But she gave great trouble to Snick-snack-snorum, whom for shortness we will call Snick-snack sometimes, though her real name was Snick-snack-snorum. For she was fond of running about, and jumping and dancing; and Snick-snack said that a King's daughter ought not to jump about like common children, but turn out her toes and walk quite slow and stately, with her parasol in the air, as she did. And Miss Snick-snack herself was a very grand young lady indeed, and carried her parasol high in the air, as well as her head, quite stately, and was so tightly laced that she could only walk three steps at a time without being out of breath. And, as she was lecturing Skip-and-jump, she dropped her pocket-handkerchief; and Skip-and-jump was going to pick it up for her, at which she was sadly shocked, and said Kings' daughters ought never to stoop to pick up anything—nor ought Kings' daughters' nurses either —nor, indeed, could she if she tried, she was so tight about the waist, as a King's daughter's nurse ought to be. And so, not knowing what was to be done, Miss Snick-snack began to cry. Skip-and-jump would have picked it up for her directly, but she dared not; and I don't know

what they would have done, had not the King's
butler, Mr. Claretjug, with his gold chain round
his neck, come out of the palace; and, though
he was both too grand and too fat to pick it up
himself, he called out a footman to put on his
white gloves and pick it up for her. And, as he
was rather fond of Snick-snack, he took her to a
seat, and tried to comfort her. And Skip-and-
jump, seeing that Snick-snack was fond of talking
to the butler, slipped away to the jackdaw to
have a chat with him.

The jackdaw soon told her of the little elf who
lived alone in the rabbit warren on the hill, and
asked her if she would not like to go and see his
little house, and where he kept his bacon. But
she said she did not know what an elf was, or
whether he would bite her if she went to see him.
And the jackdaw told her that an elf was a sort
of funny little wee-wee man, so small that he
had fitted up a nice little house in a rabbit hole,
and was very fond of nice little girls; but that
he was very lonely for want of a companion,
having nobody but the rabbits to talk to. And
Skip-and-jump said she would be very glad to go
and see him, but she did not know whether the
King her papa, and the Queen her mamma, would
approve of it; and she was sure her nurse, Snick-
snack-snorum, could not walk so far, and would

not let her go alone. So the jackdaw said she
must ask the King her papa, and the Queen her
mamma, at dessert, if she might go, and if they
gave her leave, he would try to manage about
Snick-snack-snorum. And now, as they were
talking, the butler, Mr. Claretjug, with his gold
chain about his neck, came up, and, making a low
bow to the King's daughter, said that Miss
Snick-snack requested her Royal Highness to
leave the society of that low jackdaw and come
and resume her walk. So Skip-and-jump, who
always did as she was told, went to Snick-snack,
who had now recovered from her agitation ; and
they walked once round the yard, very slow and
stately, with their parasols in the air, and then
went in that Skip-and-jump might dress for dessert. And, when she went in to dessert, the
King and Queen were sitting on their gold
thrones at the table, with their gold crowns on
their heads, and their sceptres in their hands, the
King dressed in gold and the Queen in silver,
and were eating fruit out of gold plates, and
drinking wine out of diamond glasses, which the
butler, with his gold chain, poured out for them.
And all the lords and ladies were standing around
them very grandly dressed. And Skip-and-jump
sat down on a little golden chair, and had some
fruit off a little golden plate, and some wine out

of a little diamond glass, that was made on purpose for her; and then she told the King and
Queen what the jackdaw had told her about the
little elf, and asked if she might go and see him.

The Queen said that she feared the jackdaw
was a queer sort of fellow, and not used to good
society; and that, as to the elf, she knew nothing
about him, and did not know what to say about
it. But the King said that he knew the jackdaw
very well, and he was a very good fellow, and
that, as to the elf, he might be a good fellow too;
and, if he was so lonely, he did not see why
their daughter should not go and try to cheer him
up a bit. And the Queen said that at any rate
she must not go unless Snick-snack approved of
it; for she had the greatest confidence in Snick-
snack, having chosen her as nurse out of fifty
young ladies who had offered for the place, because she thought her so very genteel. So it
was agreed that Skip-and-jump might go to see
the elf if Snick-snack approved of it; and then
the Queen was carried to bed by seven duchesses: for she was such a grand Queen that she
never walked at all, but always had to be carried
by duchesses, except when she rode in her glass
coach. But the King sat still at the table on his
throne drinking his wine; and Skip-and-jump
gave him a kiss, and skipped away to bed.

Next day, when Skip-and-jump had done her lessons, she went out again with Snick-snack, who again told her to turn out her toes, and carry her parasol high in the air, and walk slow and stately. And Skip-and-jump did as she was told, but she did not like it at all; for she longed to skip away to talk to the jackdaw. And the jackdaw was watching them all the time, standing on one leg, and winking with one eye, and thinking how he could manage the matter. So he hopped away to the butler's pantry, where the butler, with his golden chain on, had just fallen asleep in his chair over a wing of partridge which he was eating. And the jackdaw hopped upon the table, and, setting up a great caw, which woke the butler, ran off with his partridge wing into the yard. And the butler got up in a rage, and followed the jackdaw into the yard, where he ran against Skip-and-jump and Snick-snack, and nearly knocked them down. And then Mr. Claretjug stayed to talk to Snick-snack; and so Skip-and-jump was able again to skip away to talk to the jackdaw.

"Now," said the jackdaw, "those two are very happy together, and we can slip away to see the elf, and nobody will stop us."

But Skip-and-jump said she might not go

without Snick-snack's leave, as the Queen her
mamma had told her.

" Well," said the jackdaw, " then go and ask
her, and I don't think she'll refuse you now."

So she went to ask Snick-snack, who said,
" Certainly, my dear, as the Queen has said so."

So Skip-and-jump and the jackdaw left them
sitting on the seat, and tripped off merrily to the
rabbit warren on the hill to find the little elf.

CHAPTER II.

WHEN they got to the hill, they saw plenty of
little rabbits playing at hide-and-seek in and
out of their holes.   And Jack asked them if
they knew whether the elf was at home.   And
they said they believed he was taking a nap after
his dinner, but that, if they called to him at the
door of his house, he would very likely come out
and speak to them.   His house was quite at the
top of the hill, and the entrance to it was a little
rabbit hole, over which the elf had built a grand
little portico of sods and branches, with chestnuts
and fir-cones hung over it for ornament.   And
Jackdaw put his head inside the portico and set
up a caw three times.   This brought the elf out

rubbing his eyes, as if he had been asleep. He
was a funny looking little fellow, very small indeed, or he could not have lived inside a rabbit
hole ; and he kept wagging his head about, and
straddled with his legs, and wore red trousers,
and a blue jacket, and a feather in his cap. And
as soon as he saw the Princess, he knew who it
was, and took his cap off, and made a bow, and
said he felt greatly honoured by her visit. And
Skip-and-jump said she had come to see him,
because the jackdaw had said he was so lonely,
and she would be so much obliged to him if he
would show her his little house, and where he
kept his bacon. To which he replied, that his
poor little house was not fit for a King's daughter
to go into, but that her wishes were his com-
mands. So they went in all three together.

How Skip-and-jump got in I don't know, for
the entrance was only a rabbit hole, and she was
bigger than that ; but I suppose the elf, who was
wonderfully clever, managed it some way. The
house was a very nice little house after all when
they got into it ; for the elf, with the help of the
rabbits, had hollowed several rooms out of the
earth, and carpeted them with the skins of moles,
and papered them with birch-tree bark, all white,
and put tables in made of fir-cones, and chairs
and sofas covered with soft moss ; and there were

little dishes made of walnut-shells, for the elf to eat out of, and cups made of acorns for him to drink out of; and they had caught several will-o'-the-wisps in the marshes, and tied them to the ceiling to give light in the room. And against the wall was hanging the elf's little wee-wee fiddle, and there were pictures against the wall which the elf himself had painted.

Among them were two pictures, one of a beautiful lady, and the other of a beautiful gentleman, that looked like a King and a Queen; and, when Skip-and-jump asked him who they were, the elf said they were his papa and mamma. And she wondered how it was that such a beautiful papa and mamma could have such a little son, and such a funny looking one; but she was too polite to say anything. And there was another picture of a beautiful Princess, and she asked who that was. But the elf only wagged his head backwards and forwards, and said he could not tell her. And the jackdaw all the time stood on the back of a chair, winking with one eye, and looking very knowing. But he said nothing. And when she had seen all this, Skip-and-jump said she would like, above all things, to see where he kept his bacon, that the jackdaw had told her about. So he took her into a little room, where his bacon was hanging

up, and all sorts of good things besides, spar-
rows, and oranges, and apples, and cherry pies,
for the elf to eat. Then the elf said he would
show her how the rabbits could dance. And he
called a lot of rabbits in, and took his little fiddle
down, and played to them ; and they danced all
about the room, and jumped on each other's
backs, and stood on their heads, and waggled
their hind legs and their little tails in time to the
music. And the elf danced too, and waggled his
head about, and kicked his little red legs about;
and all was so funny that Skip-and-jump laughed
till her sides ached. At last she said it was time
to go away, for, if she stayed longer, Snick-
snack would be angry. And the elf said,
" Bother Snick-snack !"

Then Skip-and-jump said she only wanted one
thing more, and that was that he would tell her
his name. But he said he could tell it her only
on one condition, that she would marry him and
be his little wife. She replied that she could
never marry such a little man as he was; for,
when she grew up she would be a tall young
lady, and he would never grow any bigger than
he was, she supposed : besides, she was sure
Snick-snack would never approve of it, and she
did not think the Queen her mamma would. At
which the elf said again, " Bother Snick-snack !"

And Skip-and-jump told him he ought not to
say that, for it was not polite ; and her mamma
said Snick-snack was a very superior young lady.
And the elf said he could not tell her his name,
but he hoped she would come and see him again.
So she said she would ; and she and the jackdaw
went away. And, as they went, the elf stood
under his little portico, bowing, and bowing, and
bowing, with his little cap and feather in his
hand, so that she could not help laughing, he
looked so funny.

Well, another day, the butler having come into
the yard to keep Snick-snack company, Skip-
and-jump and the jackdaw set off again to see
the little elf. This time he seemed to have expected them, for he had got spick and span new
clothes on, new red trousers and a new blue
jacket, and a new white feather in his cap. And
when they came up he was all over smiles, and
waggled his head, and bowed in the most polite
way possible. And he showed Skip-and-jump
into a quite new room in the rabbit warren,
which he said he had fitted up, with the help of
the rabbits, for her dressing-room. And there he
left her that she might rest and change her dress.
It was a charming little dressing-room ; all the
walls were hung over with little white rabbits'
tails, and there were twenty will-o'-the-wisps

hanging from the ceiling. And on a table there were all sorts of beautiful dresses for Skip-and-jump to put on, and necklaces and earrings, and bracelets, and rings, and gloves, and pocket-handkerchiefs, and satin shoes, and everything you could think of. And she jumped about with delight, and wondered where he could have got them all. She was a long time choosing what she should wear ; but at last she dressed herself as fine as she could, and went out, with rings on every finger, and a diamond necklace round her neck, and with a frock of gold gauze covered with diamonds, to join the elf and the jackdaw. Then the elf led her into the dining-room, where there was a splendid lunch set out ; such good stuff to eat! And Skip-and-jump wondered whether it had all come out of the place where he kept his bacon. But she liked nothing so much as the cherry pie with cream. And the jackdaw had a dish of cherries all to himself, which he enjoyed very much, and said Ca, ca, ca, which meant, " This is a jolly place to feed at." When lunch was over, the rabbits came in again and danced, and the elf played his fiddle, and danced too, and Skip-and-jump laughed till her sides ached.

When she was going away, she again asked him to tell her his name ; but he said he could

not, unless she would marry him. But she again
said she could not, at which the elf looked sad,
and said he could not tell her his name; but this
time he did not say, " Bother Snick-snack," because she had asked him not. So she promised
to come again if she could, and went away with
the jackdaw.

CHAPTER III.

WHEN they got back to the King's palace, they
found Snick-snack and Mr. Claretjug still sitting
on the seat together. And Snick-snack, seeing
how fine the little Princess was dressed, asked
her where she had got all those fine things. And
Skip-and-jump told her that the elf had lots more
of them, and that she might have as many as she
wished for ; and Snick-snack, who was very fond
of dress, said she would like to go there too, and
began to cry because she could not walk so far.
Then Skip-and-jump told what good things
there had been to eat, and particularly the cherry
pie and cream, and that there was lots more
in the place where he kept his bacon. And then
the butler, who was very fond of eating, said he
would like to go there too, and almost blubbered

because he could not walk so far. So Snick-snack sat fanning herself and crying; and Claret-jug sat mopping his face with his red silk pocket-handkerchief, and almost blubbering; and Skip-and-jump stood staring at them with her large blue eyes, and almost laughing; and jackdaw stood winking at them with one eye, in a comical way.

At last a thought seemed to strike Mr. Claret-jug, and he said he would get the King's coachman to lend them the pony chaise, and they would drive there to-morrow. But it was a long time before he thought of this, for he was a slow thinker. And then Snick-snack dried her eyes, and took the Princess in to dress for dessert. And, next day, the coachman lent them the pony chaise, and Skip-and-jump asked if she might run on before with the jackdaw; and Snick-snack was very glad to let her, for she wanted all the room she could get in the carriage, and she took up so much room that the butler could hardly get in beside her; and when he had squeezed himself in at last, he was very uncomfortable. So Skip-and-jump ran on before, and told the elf they were coming, and he begged her to step into her dressing-room and he would receive them; and he said this with a wink and a sly look, as if he had some fun in his head. So, when they came, he was standing in his portico, and made a bow to them. But the butler, smelling the eatables through the rabbit hole, was in such a hurry to get at them that he took no notice of the elf, but rushed headlong at the hole, which was so small that there he stuck fast, and could neither get back nor forward. And Snicksnack was in such a hurry to get to the fine dresses that she stumbled over the butler, and was so tightly laced that she could not get up again; and so there she lay sprawling. And all the rabbits came and gambolled over Snick-snack, and spoilt her dress with their little dirty feet; and the elf danced a hornpipe on the butler, and hurt his stomach. But Skip-and-jump, hearing the noise, came out to see what was the matter, and begged the elf to let them get up again. And she and the elf and the jackdaw helped them up again, and they were both in a great rage and would not stay; and Snick-snack said that Skip-and-jump must go home directly. And Snick-snack told the Queen such a dreadful tale about the elf's behaviour, that the Queen said her daughter should go there no more. So for several years she saw the poor little elf no more, nor the jackdaw; for Snick-snack would not let her walk in the yard again, but only in the garden, where the jackdaw was not allowed to come.

And there they walked every day, with their parasols in the air, and turning out their toes, very slow and stately. But Skip-and-jump did not like it at all, and longed to see the elf and the jackdaw. ⁀

At last she grew to be a beautiful young lady; and the King and Queen said it was time she got married. And they wanted her to marry an old King called Cophetua, who was very rich, but had a hooked nose and green eyes. And Skip-and-jump said she would not marry him; and they did not know what to do with her. So one day, as the Queen was going to drive out in her glass coach, she thought she would take the Princess with her, to see if change of air would do her good. So the seven duchesses carried the Queen into the coach, and Skip-and-jump sat down beside her, in her primrose gloves, and her parasol, looking very beautiful; and she wore round her neck the diamond necklace that the elf had given her. And it so happened that they drove past the hill where the rabbit warren was; and Skip-and-jump asked the Queen if she might just run up and see whether the elf was alive still. And the Queen, wishing to humour her daughter, and because she was too grand a Queen to take the trouble to hinder her, said she might go, but she was not to be long. So she jumped out of

the glass coach and ran up the hill; and all the
rabbits saw her, and came to welcome her.
But they all looked very sad, and said the elf
was in a very bad way, and she was only just in
time to save him. She found him lying in his
portico looking very pale and poorly, and so
weak that he could hardly speak.

"Dear old elf," said the Princess, "what *is*
the matter with you, and what can I do for you?
and will you please tell me your name?"

And the elf was just able to say that he could
not tell her his name unless she would say she
would marry him. So the Princess, being very
curious to know his name, and thinking she would
rather marry him than the old King with the
green eyes, and besides being very sorry for the
elf, said she would. And all at once he changed
into a young Prince, quite tall and handsome:
and he told her his name was "Prince Ring-
rang-rong-aroo," and that he was the son of the
King of Babylon, and that a wicked old fairy,
whom he had refused to marry, had once cast a
spell upon him, that he should become a little elf
and live by himself in a rabbit warren, till some
beautiful Princess would consent to marry him;
and that he had always hoped a Princess would
come some day, and had painted a picture of
such a one as he should like, the picture she had

seen in his house; and that, if she would go in, she would see it was just like herself. And she went in and saw it, and it was just like her, though she had no idea before she was so beautiful. And then she took the Prince down the hill to the Queen, who was waiting impatiently in her glass coach. And the Queen was quite pleased with the Prince's look, and, when she heard he had such a grand name, and was the son of the King of Babylon, she said her daughter might marry him and welcome. And the King gave his consent too, and they had a very grand wedding. The jackdaw was asked to the wedding, and ate cherries at it out of a golden dish; and the old crow and his wife were asked too, but they had grown too old to come.

When the King and Queen died, the Prince and Princess became King and Queen; and, when she was Queen, she refused to be carried about by duchesses as the old Queen had been, but always walked and skipped about as before; which so shocked Mr. Claretjug and Miss Snick-snack-snorum, that they gave up their places and got married, and lived in a grand house which the young Queen gave them, by themselves. And the butler did nothing but eat; and he ate so much that at last he burst, and there was an end of him. And Snick-snack-snorum did no-

thing but dress; and one day she laced her stays
so tight that she broke in two, and there was an
end of her.

But the jackdaw always lived with the young
King and Queen, who reigned for a long time
very happily together, by the names of King
Ring-rang-rong-aroo and Queen Skip-and-jump-
ina.

THE ADVENTURES OF TOMMY TOD-GERS AND JEMMY JUMPER IN THE WOOD.

OMMY Todgers and Jemmy Jumper were two little boys. Tommy Todgers said to Jemmy Jumper, " Let's have a lark."

" O yes," said Jemmy Jumper, " let's kill the cat."

So they set three terrier dogs to worry the poor cat.

" What shall we do next ?" said Tommy Todgers.

" Let's eat all Mr. Goodman's apples," said Jemmy Jumper.

So they climbed into Mr. Goodman's apple tree, and ate his apples.

" What shall we do next ?" said Jemmy Jumper.

" Let's roll in the mud and spoil our clothes," said Tommy Todgers.

So they rolled in the mud and spoiled their clothes.

"And now," said Tommy Todgers, "let us go into the wood and get nuts."

"O yes," said Jemmy Jumper. And he put his hands on Tommy Todgers' shoulders, and jumped over his head, and away he ran to the wood, and Tommy ran after him, and they were soon there.

They found lots of nuts and ate them till they were quite full and sleepy. "I feel my waistcoat very tight," said Tommy.

"I couldn't jump over you now, if I tried," said Jemmy; "and I wish I was in bed."

"Let us go to bed here," said Tommy, "for it's too dark now to find the way home."

So they lay down under a tree, and fell asleep. They had not been asleep long, when the nightingale began to sing. And they heard her in their dreams, and thought it was Tommy's sister, little Lucy, singing. So they slept all the sounder, and had pleasant dreams.

By-and-by, the mice came out of their holes, and began to play; and they ran over the little boys' faces, and nibbled at their ears; and Tommy woke up, and thought Jemmy was pinching him; so he gave him a cuff, and Jemmy gave Tommy another; and then they fell asleep again. But they did not sleep so comfortably after this: for the mice kept squeaking in their ears, and running over their faces, and nibbling at them. And they kept waking up, and cuffing each other; but when they heard the nightingale sing, they fell asleep again. By-and-by the great brown owl, who lived in the hollow tree under which they were sleeping, woke up, and flew out silently with his great soft wings, and swooped down upon the mice, and ate several of them up in a moment; and all the other mice ran away, frightened to death, and hid themselves in their holes. But the great brown owl stood staring at the two little boys. And when he saw they were fast asleep, he said, "To whoo, to whoo!" as loud as he could, to waken them. And the nightingale gave over singing, and nothing was to be heard in the wild wood but the great brown owl shouting, "To whoo, to whoo!" This noise again woke the little boys, and they started up, and oh! how frightened they were when they saw the great brown owl's two huge round eyes, like two great fires, staring at them. They wished they had never come into the wood to eat nuts; and they felt how naughty they had been to come: for their mamas had not given them leave, and did not know where they were. But there they were lying trembling on the ground, with the great brown owl's huge round eyes like fires staring at them.

"Please, sir, don't eat us up," said Tommy Todgers.

"I'll do so no more," said Jemmy Jumper.

But the owl only said, "To whoo."

"Very well thank you, sir," said Tommy Todgers; for he thought the owl meant, "How do you do?"

But the owl did not answer, and went on staring at them for a very long time, till the little boys could not speak for fear.

At last they saw a little wee wee man come up to the owl; and they thought, "This must be an elf." And so he was. And he said to the owl, "What do you mean, you great stupid brown thing, by silencing the nightingale, who was singing to my fairy Princess, with your ugly To whoo?" And he gave the owl a kick, and the owl flew away very sulky into his hole in the tree. And then the elf went up to the two little boys, grinning with his queer wide mouth from ear to ear.

"Now, little chaps," he said, "you must get up and come with me, for I've got something for you to do." And he gave them both a kick to stir them up; and they got up terribly frightened, and followed the elf. He led them to a little cave which was his house, and asked them if they were hungry.

And they said, " No, for they had eaten nuts till they were quite full, and their waistcoats felt very tight, which they knew was a sign they had had enough."

" That's lucky," said the elf, " for, if so, there'll be no time lost. Now, do what I tell you, or I'll bring the great brown owl to eat you both up as he did the mice. In the honeysuckle bower yonder, where you see the glowworms, lies the Fairy Princess asleep. I want to marry her, but she won't have me, because I have such a wide mouth. I dare not go near her, for she has a guard of wasps round her, who come out and sting me. You, Tommy Todgers, must go and watch close to her bower, and let me know as soon as she wakes ; and, if the wasps sting you, you must not mind. And now, Jemmy Jumper, I'll tell you what *you* must do. In yonder thorn bush is the nightingale I had hired to sing to the Fairy Princess while she sleeps, for she likes nothing so much. But that great, stupid, brown owl has frightened the nightingale ; so you must climb up into the thorn bush, and ask her very prettily to sing again. I would go, but the thorns would prick me. If they prick you, you must not mind. Off with you both, and I'll stay here and smoke my pipe."

So the elf lighted his pipe, and sat in his cave grinning with his wide mouth and smoking, and the little boys were obliged to do as he told them.

First I'll tell you what Jemmy Jumper did. He went and tried to climb up the thorn bush where the nightingale was, but the thorns pricked him so that he cried. But he was so afraid of the elf and the brown owl that he went on, and he got to the top at last, and found the nightingale.

"Please, Miss Nightingale," he said, "will you sing one of your pretty songs again; for the elf has sent the owl to bed, and he won't frighten you any more."

When the nightingale heard that, she began to sing; and she sang so beautifully, that Jemmy Jumper forgot his scratches, and sat in the bush quite delighted with the music.

As for Tommy Todgers, he crept on tiptoe to the honeysuckle bower where the Fairy Princess was, very much afraid of the wasps. And well he might be; for, when he came to the bower, they flew out, buzzing round his face, and stung him. But he dared not go back for fear of the elf and the owl; so he stood still crying, And when the wasps saw that he stood still and made no noise, they flew back, and gave over stinging

him ; and he saw the Fairy Princess asleep in her
bower.

She was lying asleep on a bed of honeysuckle
leaves, and she had a crown of dewdrops on, and
a green gossamer dress, and the little bees were
singing lullaby round her, and the little moths
were fanning her with their wings. And Tommy
thought her so beautiful that he stood staring
at her with his mouth open, and forgot his
stings.   And, when the nightingale began to
sing again, she smiled in her sleep as if she was
pleased, and looked more beautiful than before.

After a long time she woke, and saw Tommy
Todgers, who set off running to tell the elf she
was awake.   But she sent the wasps after him to
bring him back ; and they came buzzing about
his face, and stung him and stung him till he
turned round and went back to the Princess,
though he did so with great fear lest the elf
should make the great brown owl eat him for not
doing as he had been told.   Then the Princess
told him he ought not to have run away, for she
wanted to keep him to be her train-bearer.
" But," said she, " you're too fat ; you look as if
you had eaten too many apples and nuts ; you
must be thinned down while I have another
sleep.   Thin him down, wasps."

So she lay down to sleep again, and the wasps

came buzzing about Tommy and made him run as hard as he could round the outside of the honeysuckle bower, till he nearly dropped, and whenever he lagged one of them stung him. This made him quite thin. And by the time he had got thin, the Princess woke again, and called for him, and asked him where he had come from. And he told her about the owl and the elf. And she said the elf was a little wide-mouthed monster, and she would play him a trick presently. Then Tommy told her about Jemmy Jumper being sent by the elf up the thorn bush to ask the nightingale to sing, and how he was afraid the elf might make the owl eat him, as the nightingale had now given over singing. So the Princess laughed, and sent an army of bats to bring Jemmy out of the thorn bush, if he was still there.

In a pretty pickle they found him. For the nightingale had sung till she was tired, and had flown away; and when the elf heard that she had stopped, he had straddled to the bottom of the thorn bush, with his pipe in his mouth, and shouted to Jemmy Jumper to come down, that he might lick him for letting the nightingale go away. And Jemmy was trying to get down— though he was terribly afraid of the elf—but the thorns pricked him when he tried, and ran into his stomach, which was swelled out with eating too many apples and nuts. So the bats put their leather wings under him, and lifted him up, and flew away with him to the Fairy Princess's bower. And, when she saw him, she said he was too fat, and told the wasps to thin him as they had done Tommy Todgers. And, when he was thin enough, she said he was to be her second train-bearer.

"And now," she said, "we'll go and have some fun with that wide-mouthed little villain, the elf, who must be punished for his impudence in wanting me to marry him. Marry *him*, indeed!"

So she sent two little mice to tell the elf she was coming to see him. And the elf was quite delighted, and threw his pipe aside, and stuck his long fingers through his hair, to make it stick up and look smart, and stood grinning from ear to ear to receive the Princess. And the Princess set off in her green dress, and her crown of dew-drops, with Tommy Todgers and Jenny Jumper carrying her train. And her guard of wasps flew before her; and the moths fanned her with their wings as she walked, and the little bees hummed music; and the flowers bowed under her feet, and gave out their sweetest scents. And when she came to the elf's cave she sat

down in a stately way, and the elf stood grinning
with his great wide mouth, and bowing.

" It was a very pretty little serenade that you
have been giving me to night," said the Princess
to the elf, " and it was very kind of you to hire
the nightingale to sing to me : but couldn't you
sing yourself; for I had rather hear you than
any nightingale."

Now, she only said this to make fun of the
elf; but he thought she was in earnest, such a
vain little monster as he was.   So he said he was
very hoarse, but to please her he would try to
sing.   And he opened his great mouth so wide
that you could see all down his throat; and he
made such faces, and sang in such a hoarse
voice, without any tune, that the Princess burst
out laughing; and Tommy Todgers and Jemmy
Jumper could not help laughing too.   And, when
his mouth was wide open, she gave a sign to the
wasps, who flew into his throat and stung him.
And the elf screamed horribly, and rolled head
over heels, grinning and howling.   And the
Princess laughed with a voice like silver, and
Tommy and Jemmy could not help laughing too,
so that they jerked her train so much that she
told them to be quiet, or the wasps should sting
them.   And then she pretended to the elf that
the wasps had flown into his throat without her

leave, and said she hoped he was not much hurt. And he made the best of it with a very wry face, and said he would do anything to please her.

So she asked him to dance. And he said that he was very stiff in the legs, but that he would try. So he began to dance, with his little straddling bandy legs, and with his great wide mouth grinning all the time at the Princess, and with his long thin arms waving in the air, as he snapped his fingers. And he looked so ridiculous that the Princess burst out laughing again in her silver voice, and Tommy and Jemmy laughed as much as they dared under her green train.

Then the Princess made a sign to the mice, who ran among the elf's feet as he danced, and nibbled at them till he squeaked; and at last they tripped him up, and he lay sprawling on the ground. And then the mice ran over his back and nibbled at him, and the wasps flew round his head and stung him, till he kicked and howled and did not know what to do.

So when the Princess thought he was punished enough, she got up and told Tommy and Jemmy to lift up her train, as she tripped away again to her honeysuckle bower, with the guard of wasps going before her, and the moths fanning her with their wings, and the bees singing to her, and the flowers bowing before her. And, when she got there, she asked Tommy and Jemmy how they liked living in Fairy land. And they said they liked carrying her train very much, she was so beautiful, and smelt so sweet of honeysuckle; but they were dreadfully afraid of the owl and the elf, and hoped she would not let the wasps sting them any more. And she said the elf would have had no power over them, nor the owl either, if they had been good boys, and not come into the wood without leave, and eaten too many nuts, and that she never let the wasps sting really good boys; for the fairies were very fond of good boys, and were always kind to them. And then she asked them about Tommy Todgers' little sister Lucy, and whether she would like to come and be her lady in waiting. And the little boys were just thinking how nice it would be if they and Lucy could come and live there always with the Fairy Princess in the honeysuckle bower, when the sun began to rise; and, all on a sudden, they saw the Princess no more, but only a flower of honeysuckle, round which the moths were fluttering and the bees humming. So they ran through the wood as fast as they could, and kept looking back at the tree where the owl lived, fearing lest he should see them. And at last they found their way home, and told Lucy all they had seen. But she did not believe them, till they showed her how they were scratched and stung. And still she did not feel sure that all they told her was true. For she had never seen an elf or a fairy. But Tommy Todgers and Jemmy Jumper were always good boys after that night, and never went to the wood again without leave, and never ate too many nuts.

PERIWINKLE AND THE FAIRIES.

A LITTLE girl, called Periwinkle, sat one evening on the floor in the drawing room, talking to the cat. The cat's name was Woosy-Poosy. Periwinkle was rubbing Woosy-Poosy's hair to bring sparkles out of it. For cats have sparks all about their coats when they are rubbed in the dark, which big grown-up people tell you is because there is electricity about them, or some such stuff with a grand name, but which little boys and girls know is because they lie so much by the fire, which gets into them; and so of course it will come out of them again.

"How I should like to sparkle all over as you do when anybody rubbed me," said Periwinkle. "I wonder why I can't."

"It's because you aren't a cat," said Woosy-Poosy.

Now, here little boys and girls will ask how it was the cat could talk. Well, she couldn't talk as people do; but she said prr, and prr-prrr, and prr-prrr-prrrr; and sometimes she said meaw, and sometimes me-e-aw, and me-e-e-aw, and sometimes ptss, or wow, or wow-ptss, and the like; and she said such things in all kinds of ways; and Periwinkle was so used to talk to the cat that she had got to know all she meant, so she could talk away with her very nicely. Her papa and mama could not understand what the cat said, nor could Jane the nurse, nor Mary the cook, nor Dumbleboy, Periwinkle's big brother. But Periwinkle could, she was so used to her. So they went on talking. "Well," said Periwinkle; "but I'm not a cat, and I shouldn't like to be a cat, for all your sparkles."

"And why wouldn't you like to be a cat?" said Woosy-Poosy.

"Why," said Periwinkle, "because you catch mice, and eat them alive, and I think that is very wrong and cruel."

"It's not more wrong," said Woosy-Poosy, "than Mary the cook cutting off the heads of the chickens in the yard, and roasting them for your dinner."

Periwinkle did not know what to say to that; so she thought she would talk about something else, and said, "Where do you go every evening after tea, when you sneak off to the wood, and we don't see you again till supper time?"

Said the cat, " I've a fine time of it then. I
catch the little mice as they are playing at leap-
frog under the bushes, and sometimes the little
birds, as they are practising their singing lessons
on the trees; and sometimes even a young rabbit, as it is playing at hide and seek among the
holes in the ground; and they are so good to eat
between tea and supper."

" But all that is very wrong," said Periwinkle,
" and very cruel, as I've said before."

" It would be for a little girl," said Woosy-
Poosy, " but not for a cat. And then I see such
beautiful things ! Such glow-worms, and dew-
drops glistening in the moonlight ! far brighter
than the sparkles from my back. And then on
the bit of very green grass under the roots of the
old oak, I sometimes see the fairies dancing ;
such beautiful creatures, and so fond of cats !
They often get the sparkles off my back to wear
as spangles in their hair, and their little gauze
petticoats."

" What are fairies ?" said Periwinkle ; " I never
saw any."

" You would have done," replied Woosy-
Poosy, " if you had been a cat : and that is one
disadvantage of being a little girl and not a cat,
that you cannot go into the woods at night and
see the beautiful fairies."

" How I should like to see them !" said Periwinkle. " Can't you take me with you and show
me them ?"

" Yes, to be sure," said the cat; " if you'll
come out with me to-morrow night, and take
care not to make a noise, or you'll frighten them
all away; and mind you bring some salt with
you to put on the little birds' tails, and then I
shall catch them more easily."

" No, I won't do that," said Periwinkle, " for
I don't approve of your eating live birds; but
I'll come with you and see the fairies."

So they made a bargain, that next evening,
after tea, they should slip out together, and try
to see the fairies. And when the time came,
Periwinkle went up stairs, and put on her little
straw hat with the pink ribbons, and her little
blue cloak, and put in her little pocket some
suckies to give to the fairies if she should find
them; and she and the cat went out together
into the wood.

It was a beautiful night, and the glow-worms
and the dew-drops sparkled so in the grass, just
as the cat had said, and the moon was so bright,
that Periwinkle thought she had never seen anything so beautiful. But the cat vexed her by
constantly wanting to catch the mice, and the
birds, and the young rabbits. So Periwinkle pro-

mised her a dish of good cream when they got home if she would only be a good cat that one night and not catch them. And then the cat went on quietly. But once she could not help making a spring at a pretty little nightingale singing on a branch; but she missed the bird, which flew away singing, " Jug, jug," and the cat fell off the branch again to the ground, which made her very cross, and she said " Ptss, ptsss." Then Periwinkle stroked her back till the sparkles came, and that put her in a good humour again; and they went on pleasantly together till they came to the very green bit of grass under the roots of the old oak. Then Woosy-Poosy told Periwinkle to stand quite still till the fairies came, and to make no noise at all. And so she stood for a long time, but she saw no fairies.

" Stroke my back," said Woosy-Poosy, " till the sparkles come, and then the fairies will perhaps hear me crackle, and see the sparks, and come out to get spangles."

So Periwinkle did so. And by-and-by she saw a little wee wee boy and a little wee wee girl, only as big as my thumb, and all dressed in green, peeping from behind the roots of the old oak; but, when they saw Periwinkle, they ran back again as if they were frightened.

" Stand you behind the tree where they can't

see you," said Woosy-Poosy, " and I'll lie down
and rub my back on the green grass under the
roots, and then perhaps they'll come out."

So Periwinkle did as the cat told her ; and by-
and-by she saw the fairies come out, first one,
then two, then three, then lots more, none of
them bigger than my thumb, and all in green ;
and they danced round Woosy-Poosy, and
rubbed her back, and got her sparkles, and put
them in their hair and on their gauze petticoats,
till they all glittered again, and danced round her
in a ring, with little bells jingling, which they
wore for earrings ; and Periwinkle thought she
had never seen anything so beautiful.   When
they were tired of dancing, they crowded round
Woosy-Poosy, and talked to her, and by-and-by
Woosy-Poosy came round to where Periwinkle
was behind the tree, and told her she might come
forward now, and the fairies would be glad to see
her.   " But mind you behave well," said the
cat, " for the fairies can't bear naughty girls."

So Periwinkle went round the tree on tip-
toes, and the fairies crowded round her, quite
pleased and curious to see her.   But soon they
began to shrink back, and one of them said, in a
little wee tiny voice, " There's a smell of a
naughty girl here."

"Yes," said they all, "she smells like a naughty girl; let us try her."

And they took little wee torches, and lighted them at the glow-worms in the grass, and kept putting them to Periwinkle's hands and neck, as they danced round her. And she didn't like it at all, for the torches burnt her a little, though not very badly, and she cried out, "I'm not a naughty girl; but you are very naughty fairies, and Woosy-Poosy is a very naughty cat to bring me here; let us go, for I don't like you at all now."

But they told her she must be a naughty girl, or the torches would not have burnt her, for they never burnt good girls. And the cat told her that she had better confess that she had been a naughty girl that morning, for that the fairies would be quite sure to find it out, and pinch her if she didn't. So Periwinkle was obliged to confess that she had broken a new toy that very morning, though her nurse had told her to take great care of it, and that she had pinched the baby, and had eaten three cakes which her mamma had told her would not be good for her, and done other very naughty things. So the fairies danced round her again, and poked at her with their torches, laughing with little silver voices, and with all their bells jingling, till she began to cry.

Then they stopped, and told her to be a very good girl next day, and then she might come again and go into their palace, and see their Queen.

"Why can't I see her to-night?" said Periwinkle.

"Because," they replied, "she never sees naughty girls; and, besides, you could not get in, for to get in you will have to grow small like a fairy, and only good girls can do that."

So Periwinkle went home again with Woosy-Poosy, and gave her the dish of cream she had promised her, and when her mamma asked her where she had been, said she had been for a walk in the wood with Woosy-Poosy, but did not like to say anything about the fairies. And her mamma said that was all right, for Woosy-Poosy was a steady well behaved cat, and a good companion for her. And so Periwinkle went to bed.

Next morning she got up resolved to be a very good girl all the day. And so she was. She took care of all her toys, and was kind to the baby, and ate nothing but what was good for her, and did all she was told. And both her mamma, and Jane the nurse, were quite pleased with her, and said that Woosy Poosy was a very good companion for her, and had given her good advice. So, after tea, she asked her mamma if she

might have another walk in the wood with
Woosy-Poosy, and her mamma said " Yes."
So she again got her little straw hat with the
pink ribbons, and her little blue cloak, and filled
her pockets with suckies, and she and the cat set
off again to the wood.

When they came to the bit of very green grass,
under the roots of the old oak, there were the
fairies waiting for them ; and where they had
danced the night before there was a ring of grass
greener than all the rest. And they all danced
round her again, with their earrings jingling ;
and they all sung out in chorus, with little silvery
voices, " O, what a good girl she smells like
now !" And they lighted their torches at the
glow-worms again, and this time they did not
burn her at all, but felt quite cool and pleasant.
And then the fairies clambered up her blue cloak,
and kissed her, and told her she might now come
into their palace and see their Queen. So they
took her beneath the roots of the old oak, and
one of them held up a little wee wee green mantle made of gossamer, and put it over her ; and
all at once she became quite small like the
fairies ; and she crept with them through a very
little hole under the oak, which was the entrance
into the palace, where the Queen lived. It was
such a pretty little palace ! It was built of beau-

tiful little shells, and lighted all over with glow-
worms' tails, and dewdrops sparkled all over it
like diamonds, and all the ground was covered
with beautiful tiny flowers of all sorts of bright
colours, and there were little roses and honey-
suckles overhead.

But Periwinkle did not yet see the Queen.
And the fairies showed her a curtain of pink rose
leaves, and said that inside that curtain was the
Queen's dressing-room, where she was dressing
for the ball, and that Periwinkle must wait until
Her Majesty was ready to receive strangers. So
she waited, and saw beautiful little fairies creeping in and out of the pink curtain, carrying in
the things the Queen was going to wear. One was
running in with sparkles off the cat's back, to put
in the Queen's hair; another with a chain woven
out of moon-beams for her to wear round her
neck; and the little wren, both the cock and the
hen, were pulling the feathers out of their
breasts to put into the Queen's fan, which a fairy
made and carried in; and the beetle, with his
thread and needle, was finishing the Queen's
gauze petticoat made of gossamer, and spangled
over with colours off butterflies' wings; and,
this, when it was finished, another fairy carried
in. And then a fairy said that the Queen took
a long time dressing, and would not be ready

yet, and offered, in the meantime, to show Periwinkle the place where they kept the presents
that they gave to good little girls and boys at
Christmas. And lo! there they all were, packed
up in shells against the walls, and there was the
little boy's or the little girl's name for whom they
were meant, written over each shell. And there
were thousands of these shells. And Periwinkle
wondered to see such lots of things packed into
a single little shell—dolls, books, horses, tops,
balls, sucky-boxes, Noah's arks, and all kinds of
things. But the fairies told her that all these
things grew bigger when they got into the houses
where the little boys and girls lived, and that
they were very small now because they were in
Fairy land.

Soon, peering about, she spied an empty shell,
with her own name over it, and she asked what
that meant; and the fairies told her that out of
that shell had come all the pretty things the fairies
had sent her last Christmas, and that they had
not filled it again, because she had so often been
a naughty girl, and they never began to fill the
shells till the little boys and girls were good.
Then she spied another shell, full of pretty
things, with her big brother Dumbleboy's name
over it. And they told her that those had been
meant for Dumbleboy last Christmas, but he had

been so naughty just before Christmas came that
they had not sent them, but he would get them
next Christmas if he was good. And Periwinkle
remembered that Dumbleboy had killed the other
cat, and stuck pins into Jane the nurse, and
pulled the baby's nose, and made himself ill with
fat rascals, just before last Christmas, and had got
no presents from the fairies. And now, as they
were looking about, the beetle, with his thread
and needle, set up a great hum; and the fairies
said that it was a signal that the Queen was
dressed, and Periwinkle might go in to see her.
So they had to creep under the rose leaf curtain,
and she found herself in the Queen's dressing-
room, rather frightened, for she had never seen a
Queen, and wondered what she would do to her.

The room was lined all over with rose leaves,
and three little gilded flies were singing a glee,
with a daisy before them for a music-stand, for
the Queen's amusement, and the Queen herself
was reclining on a couch of rose leaves at the end
of the room, and two gentlemen fairies were fanning her with little butterfly's wings, for she was
hot with the fatigue of dressing; and another, on
his knee, was offering her a draught of dew out
of a fairy cup; and a lady fairy was scenting the
Queen's tiny gossamer pocket-handkerchief with
juice out of a leaf of honeysuckle, which the

Queen took in her hand when she had buttoned
her tiny white gloves, and waved it to Periwinkle, as a sign that she might come and talk to
her. And Periwinkle went up to her, and the
Queen said she was very glad to see her, and
that, as she was such a good girl, she might
dance with the fairies that night. And then the
King came, dressed in armour made of green
beetles' wings, and took the Queen by the hand,
and led her out, and danced with her. As they
danced, a band of grasshoppers, sitting on a toad-
stool, chirped music all the time, and the fairies'
bells jingled in time with the music. And when
the King had danced with the Queen, he came
and danced with Periwinkle. And when he had
danced with her, the King's son came and offered
her his hand. He was a beautiful fairy, dressed
in clothes made out of the wings of little green
flies, and Periwinkle loved him very much, and
was quite pleased to dance with him. And when
they had danced a long time, the King's son told
her that he loved her very much, and asked her
to stay and live there, and be his little wife; and
she was just going to say yes, when she heard
Woosy-Poosy, who was lying on her back under
the roots of the old oak all the time, say,
" Meaw-prr." And she knew what that meant;
and she told the King's son that she could not

leave her papa and mamma. And the King's
son said that it was a great bore; for that, if she
married him, she would have to come and live
there always. And they were both very sorry,
and could not tell what was to be done. But the
King's son said that, if anybody could tell them
what was to be done, it was the old mole, who
lived in a deep hole not far off, and who was a
hundred years old, and blind, and had grown
wiser than anybody else from burrowing so long
underground. "Nobody had gone so deep as he
had," said the King's son.

So they slipped away from the fairy ring, and
went to find the old mole. First they had to go
down a little hole in the ground, and then they
had to find their way underground through long
dark passages, to get to the cell at the end where
the mole lived. And Periwinkle got frightened;
but the King's son put his arm round her waist,
and then she felt better again. At last they got
at the old mole; but he was in a bad humour,
for he had just been nearly caught in a mole-
trap (for all his wisdom), and had lost a bit of
his tail; besides, he had burrowed by himself so
long that he could not speak. They asked him
a lot of questions, but they could get nothing
out of him but grunts. So they went away again.

"Ah!" said the King's son, "if he could but

have spoken, we should have learnt everything.
But, if the old mole cannot tell us what is to be
done, perhaps the old owl can, who lives in the
hollow of the elm tree, and who, instead of being
blind, can see in the dark, and who is said to
be two hundred years old, and who has grown
wiser even than the mole, from looking so long
at the stars. " No one has seen so far as he has,"
said the King's son.

So they went to find the old owl. And again
Periwinkle got frightened, for they had to clamber
up the tall elm tree, and she was afraid of falling.
But the King's son put his arm round her waist,
and then she felt better. At last they came to
the hollow of the tree where the old owl lived.
And they asked him all kinds of questions; but
he only looked at them with his great staring
eyes, which were so sharp that they went right
through them, so that he did not see them at all,
but only the stars; and all he said was " To-
whoo!" And so they could make nothing of
what he meant, and had to go down again.

" Ah! if we could but have understood what
he meant by ' To-whoo!' we should have learnt
everything," said the King's son; " but as nobody can tell us what is to be done, let us refresh
ourselves and have another dance."

So they sucked some honey out of the clover,

and drank some dew out of the fairy cups, and
then they danced again. And when the dance
was over, the King's son again asked her to be
his little wife; and she was just going to say yes,
when she heard the cat say " Meaw, meaw, prr,
prr, prrrr." And she knew what that meant, and
told the King's son again that she could not leave
her papa and mamma. But this time the King's
son was very angry, and went and told the Queen
that he had asked Periwinkle twice to be his
little wife, and that she had said she could not
leave her papa and mamma. And at first the
Queen seemed angry too, and told Periwinkle
that the Prince had done her a great honour in
asking her to be his little wife, and that she
ought not to refuse him. But Periwinkle made
a curtsey to the Queen, and said that she loved
the Prince very much, but that she could not
leave her papa and mamma. And then the Queen
said she was a good girl, but it was all very un-
fortunate, and she didn't know what was to be
done. So she made a sign to all the fairies to
stop the ball, and the crickets gave over playing,
and the bells ceased to jingle, and all the sparkles on the fairies' hair and dresses went out in a
moment. And then the Queen kissed Periwinkle,
and told her that, if she was a good girl, she
would still send her presents at Christmas, but

F

she feared she could see her no more; for they must all go to another climate, to recruit the Prince's health and spirits. And then she took the gossamer green mantle off Periwinkle's shoulders, and vanished in a moment. And Periwinkle was her own size again, and saw nothing but the cat waiting for her to go home. And they went home, and though they often came again to the old oak tree, they never found the fairies any more. But they always sent her presents at Christmas, for after that time she was always a very good girl. But the cat never gave up catching live mice and birds.

JACK VALIANT AND TIM BRAG.

THERE were once two brothers, Timothy and John, commonly called Tim and Jack, of whom Tim was the elder. Tim used to bully Jack, and make out that he was much the finer fellow of the two, saying often how strong and clever and brave he was, and what grand things he would do when he grew up to be a man. He boasted so much in this way, and gave himself such airs, that people called him Tim Brag. Jack was a quiet lad and did not say much.

One day they missed their sister Toddles, who had been playing by herself on the common. Night came on, and she did not come home. Next morning some one came and said a hideous blue dwarf had been seen the night before prowling about the common, and they all concluded that he had stolen Toddles away. Jack said directly that he would go out into the wide world and look for her.

" A pretty fellow you are," said Tim, " to go

into the wide world! What could a little muff
like you do there? You would run home frightened if you saw a mouse; I won't let you go."

"Well then," replied Jack, "if you won't let
me go, go yourself. Somebody must go to look
for poor little Toddles."

Tim in his heart did not like the idea of
going; but he was ashamed to say he was afraid.
So off went Tim, with a swagger and a bang,
whistling, to make people think he was not
afraid, after giving Jack a kick, and telling him
to mind the rabbits. He went on till evening,
and got very much tired and frightened, and
more than once thought of turning back; but he
was ashamed of returning home so soon; so he
walked slowly on till it began to grow dark, and
then sat down under a tree to eat his supper.
As he was munching away, a very little old woman came up to him, looking tired and hungry,
and asked him for a crust of bread.

"O yes," said Tim, "very likely that I will
give you my bread, when I want it all myself.
Move on, Mother Bunch, I'm not afraid of an
old cripple like you."

"Tim," said the old woman, "I did not want
you to give me bread for fear, but for kindness;
if you had given me some, it would have been
better for you. But I will do you a kindness

still. Take my stick, it will help you on your
journey ; and, as you would not give a poor old
woman a crust of bread for kindness, take care
you don't give up this stick for fear."

"I don't want your stick," said Tim, and
threw it at her, as she limped away. But it did
not hurt her, and she was soon out of sight.

Then Tim thought he might as well take the
stick, as it might be a good one to walk with ;
so he went and took it up, and climbed up into
the tree to sleep. O what a miserable night he
had ! The tree was hard, and the wind was cold,
and he heard the foxes barking, and the owls
hooting, and he was all over in a cold shiver,
frightened to death. Very little sleep did he get
that night. In the morning, when he came down
from the tree, he thought of nothing but running
home as fast as he could ; but he had quite lost
his way. And the further he went, the less he
could find it ; and when night came on again, he
was in a wild wood, he did not know where, and
again sat down under a tree, tired and terribly
frightened, to eat his supper. As he munched
away, looking about him every moment, he heard
a great roar in the wood. So he got up and ran
away as fast as his legs could carry him ; but the
roar came after him.

Soon an ugly, wicked-looking dwarf, with green

eyes, overtook him; for it was he that had made
all the noise, and told him in a loud harsh voice
to give him the stick he carried in his hand.

Tim remembered what the old woman had told
him about not giving it up to anyone for fear;
but he was far too much frightened to act on her
advice.

So he fell down on his knees before the dwarf,
and said, " O, Mr. Dwarf, take my stick, take
anything you like; only don't hurt me."

Then the dwarf took the stick, and laid it well
about Tim's shoulders, and went away laughing
horribly till the wood rang.

Again Tim crept up into a tree, and had a
more miserable night than before. This time the
foxes barked so loud, and so many of them, that
he thought he must have come to the kingdom of
the foxes, and that they would eat him up next
day. And this thought did not make him more
comfortable.

In the morning, when he came down from the
tree, there was nothing to be done but to wander
on in the hope of hitting on the way home; but
the more he tried to hit it, the further away he
went. Towards evening a hare came running
up to him, and asked for protection. She said
that she was in great danger from the foxes,
whose kingdom was close at hand; but that, if

Tim would protect her, and fight the foxes, they would both be safe, and she would help him to find what he wanted.

"But," she added, "it's a pity you have not a stick."

At first Tim thought of knocking the poor hare on the head, to show how strong and brave he was; but he bethought him that she might be of use to him, so he said, " Yes, my dear, you may walk beside me: I'm a very strong brave fellow, and under my protection you'll be quite safe; I've lost my stick unfortunately, but I'll cut another from this tree."

So they walked on together, and Tim kicked the hare when she did not go on as he liked, to show that he was stronger than she, and kept bragging how brave he was, and how well it was for her that she had met with him.

By and by, the foxes came in a great troop, all barking; and Tim ran away again directly, leaving the poor hare at their mercy, and they ate her up in a moment.

But Tim did not get off as easily as he had hoped; for the foxes soon came up to him, when they had eaten the hare, and barked round him till he yelled with fear. He told them that he would do anything they liked, if they would not hurt him. So they said they would spare his

life, if he would come and keep house for them,
and be their servant.

"O, yes," said Tim, "anything you like, if
you only won't hurt me."

So they took him to their house. It was a
cave under a rock, full of the bones, and feathers,
and hairs of the birds and animals that the foxes
had eaten, and there was a strong foxy smell
about it. And here they told Tim he must live,
and keep the house clean and tidy for them, and
have it clear of bones and feathers and quite
comfortable when they came home from hunting,
and nurse the little baby foxes, and take them up
and dandle them if they cried during the night,
and make no outcry if they bit him, and tickle the
old foxes' tails when they wanted to go to sleep,
and be particularly respectful and obedient to
the Mrs. Foxes and the Miss Foxes, who were
very snappish and particular.

Tim was only too glad to do all this, he was so
much afraid; but he had a hard time of it among
them all.

So there we will leave him for the present, and
see what Jack, his brother, was doing all the
time.

He waited for a week, and then, as Tim did
not return, he set out himself into the wide world
to look for Toddles. It happened to him as it

had done to Tim. At the close of the first day
he sat down under a tree to eat his supper; and
the little old woman came up to him, looking
hungry and tired, and asked for a crust of bread.

"A crust of bread?" said he; " yes, and welcome! and take a bit of this nice pie, too, and a
drink from this bottle of wine: I have but one
bottle, but I will gladly share it with you, for
you look hungry and tired."

" Jack," said the old woman, " you are a kind-
hearted lad. Come with me, and you shall have
better fare than this."

Then she led him a little way, till she came to
a bare rock; and she knocked three times on the
rock with her stick, and it flew open; and they
went in, and found themselves in a large hall,
beautifully clean and tidy; and in it there was a
table with a white cloth on it, covered with all
sorts of good things; and round the table were a
number of nice little girls in white frocks, who
shook hands with Jack, and welcomed him so
pleasantly! And when Jack had washed himself, and made himself tidy, in a little room that
the old lady showed him, he sat down to supper
with them all; and the little girls chatted and
laughed, and the old lady sat at the head of the
table inviting them to eat of all the good things;
and after supper they all sang together, and then

they played at hide and seek; and then Jack kissed the girls all round, and went to bed in his little room, and slept delightfully till morning.

In the morning the old lady came and woke him, and told him that it was time he had his breakfast, and started on his journey.

When he had done his breakfast, she told him that he would have many dangers to pass through before he found Toddles; but that, if he was a brave boy, he would get through them all.

"And I am sure," she added, "you are a brave boy, you were so kind to the little old woman when she seemed in distress. But take my stick, it will be of use to you; and mind you, never part with it."

Then Jack asked her who she was, and why she lived there with all those nice little girls.

"My name," she said, "is Mother Lovechild; and all these are little girls who have been lost in the woods, whom I am keeping here and teaching to be good, till I can send them home to their parents. But you must set off, for you have no time to lose."

So Jack started, and as he went away the nice little girls all stood waving their little handkerchiefs, and wishing him luck. But, when he turned round a second time to look at them, he saw nothing but the bare rock. Then on he

went, and did not feel a bit afraid; for the words
of the old lady had encouraged him, and he was
determined to find Toddles. When evening came,
he sat down, as before, under a tree to eat his
supper; and, as he ate, he heard a great roar in
the wood. But Jack did not run away as Tim
had done; but stood up bravely, shouldering
Mother Lovechild's stick. And when the ugly
wicked-looking dwarf with green eyes came up
and ordered him in a loud harsh voice to give
him the stick, Jack hit him a great thwack on
the head with it, and the dwarf ran away howling. But Jack ran after him, and told him he
must come with him and be his servant. And
the dwarf was so afraid of the stick that he obeyed,
making very ugly faces all the time. And Jack
ordered him to find a good place for him to lodge
in during the night; and the dwarf took him to a
nice little cabin in the wood, where he slept comfortably till morning; and then he trudged on,
with the stick on his shoulder and the dwarf at
his heels.

Towards evening a hare came running up, and
asked for protection. The dwarf wanted Jack to
kill the hare; but he would not; and when she
told about the danger she was in from the
foxes, whose kingdom was close at hand, he told
her not to be afraid, for he would do the best he

could to protect her; "Though," said he, "I am but a small fellow, and perhaps they will be too strong for me." As they walked along, she told him a good deal that was worth knowing: that the stick he carried was worth anything; for that all the bad dwarfs, and all the beasts of blood, knew Mother Lovechild's stick, and were afraid of it; that, if he succeeded in beating the foxes, he must seize, if he could, on the King of the Foxes, whom he might know by his large red tail, and that he would be of great use to them. She advised him also, when the foxes came, to throw the dwarf among them, so that, when they were eating him up, he might seize on the King of the Foxes, and make off without their minding him.

But Jack said that the dwarf was under his protection, and he could not behave so shabbily to him.

"Well," said the hare, "he deserves nothing better; but do as you like; only tell him he must help you to fight the foxes, or you will thrash him with your stick."

So Jack did so; and the dwarf promised him to do his best to fight the foxes.

By-and-by the foxes came in a great troop, barking and howling; and the hare crept under Jack's jacket for safety; and Jack laid about him manfully with his stick; and the dwarf did won-

ders: for he rushed about among the foxes, seizing
them with his teeth, and taking them by their
bushy tails, and whirling them in the air.   And
soon all that were not killed ran away helter-
skelter.   But Jack ran after one of them that had
a large red tail, and soon had him fast.   Then
the hare crept down from under Jack's jacket,
and told him what to do.

She said, " Make the King of the Foxes carry
you on his tail as swiftly as the wind to the kingdom of the blue dwarfs, where your sister Toddles is; and tell him to summon an army of foxes
to accompany you; and threaten him with Mother
Lovechild's stick, if he does not obey."

So Jack did as the hare told him, and seated
himself on the fox-king's tail, with the hare in
his arms; and the green-eyed dwarf ran by his
side roaring all the way; and an army of foxes
ran after them with their bushy tails in the air,
barking and howling till the air rang; and away
they went over hill and dale, till they came to the
kingdom of the blue dwarfs.   When they came
near it, they all stopped to arrange their plan;
and the hare gave them very good advice.

" Look," she said, " at yonder hills: among
them is the kingdom of the blue dwarfs; and, if
you look hard, you may see some of them playing
at leap-frog, which is their favourite game.   We

must not attack them now: for they are very
strong and vicious.   But wait till evening, when
they have had their supper, and then they will
be so tipsy and sleepy that we shall take them by
surprise, and have a better chance.   We will
creep softly up to them; and, when we are close
to them, the dwarf must set up a hideous roar,
and all the foxes must bark and howl, and without losing a moment you must rush in among
them, and the foxes must bite their legs, and you
must hammer their heads with your stick, and
the green-eyed dwarf must do what he can to
help: but take care you do not part with Mother
Lovechild's stick, for you can do nothing without that: and take care also to secure the king of
the blue dwarfs, whom you will know by the
great hump on his back, and his red cap; for,
ten to one, Toddles will have been enchanted
into some strange form, and you will not be able
to make her out, or deliver her, unless you have
the king in your power, and make him disenchant
her."

So Jack did as the hare told him.   He waited
till the blue dwarfs had done their supper, and
were all tipsy; and then crept softly up to them;
and all of a sudden they made such a noise as
never was heard, the green-eyed dwarf roaring,
and the foxes barking and howling; and then

they rushed in among them, and the foxes bit
their legs, and Jack hammered their heads with
his stick, and the green-eyed dwarf rushed against
their stomachs with his head and bit them. Soon
the blue dwarfs were all put to flight; but unfortunately Jack had not succeeded in securing
the King, who had slipped away behind a rock;
but he had managed to keep the stick, though he
had once nearly lost it in fighting with a strong
blue dwarf, who had almost wrenched it out of
his hand, and had bitten Jack's arm till the blood
ran. When the fight was over, they held a
consultation. The hare said, " What a pity it is
the King of the blue dwarfs has got away! for
without him I fear we shall never find poor Toddles; but it is lucky, at any rate, that you have
saved the stick; it is a powerful charm, and may
help us still."

Then they went all through the houses of the
blue dwarfs, and found the remains of their supper all in confusion, and broken glasses lying
about the floors; but go where they would, they
could see nothing of poor Toddles.

" Let us wait till morning," said the hare,
" perhaps we shall succeed better by daylight."

So they feasted on what was left of the dwarfs'
supper, and lay down to sleep.

Very early next morning the hare came and

woke Jack, and told him that she had been prowling about, and had found a secret chamber full of all kinds of birds, and weasels, and rabbits, and mice, who she fancied were enchanted people, and that Toddles might be among them. So Jack went with her to the secret chamber, and, when he touched the birds, and weasels, and mice, with Mother Lovechild's stick, they were all changed again to their natural forms, and turned out to be little boys and girls whom the blue dwarfs had stolen away and enchanted. But, alas! Toddles was not among them. But one of them, a sweet little girl in a blue frock, who had been the last enchanted, said that the King of the blue dwarfs had come home a few weeks ago with a new little girl, who had cried very much, and wanted to go home; and that the King had been very angry with her, and threatened to shut her up in a walnut-shell, till she would consent to live with him.

"Well, then," said the hare, "we must look about till we find a walnut-shell."

They looked all day, but could not find one. At last the hare spied a strong iron door, fastened with seven locks, on the side of a rock; and the little girl in the blue frock said she believed it led into the King's private apartments. So Jack touched the seven locks one after the other with the stick, and the door flew open, and they went in, and found a small room; but still they could see no walnut-shell. But on a shelf was a large iron box fastened with twenty locks. And Jack touched the twenty locks one after the other with the stick, and the box flew open, and inside it there was another box of steel with forty locks, and they flew open too when they were touched with the stick; and inside was another box of silver with seventy locks, which flew open like the others when they were touched with the stick; and inside that was another box of gold with a hundred locks. It was a long time before Jack got them all opened, but he did at last; and inside the golden box there was a single walnut-shell. And when Jack touched it with the stick, there was heard a feeble moan inside, and he felt sure Toddles was there. So he cracked the nut very very gently, for fear of hurting her; and there she was to be sure, so small, so very very small, that she lay quite snug in the walnut-shell. But, when she was touched with the stick, she was her proper size again, and she hardly knew what to do, she was so pleased to see her brother Jack.

Well, they were all very merry for the rest of the day; and early next morning they set off home. Jack, as before, rode on the tail of the

King of the Foxes, with the hare in his arms;
and Toddles rode beside him on the tail of another
fox; and all the little boys and girls rode on the
tails of other foxes; and the green-eyed dwarf
ran beside them, roaring as loud as he could;
and all the army of foxes barked and howled;
and away they went like the wind over hill and
dale, till the air rang with the noise./ When they
arrived at the kingdom of the foxes, the King of
the Foxes invited them all to stay and see the
lady foxes, and refresh themselves with a feast.
And Jack thanked them, and said they would be
very glad.   But the hare advised them not to go
into the foxes' cave, there would be such a foxy
smell about it: so it was arranged that the feast
should be spread outside under a tree, and the
ladies should come out to them.   And soon the
Queen Fox, and the Mrs. Foxes, and the Miss
Foxes, all came out, mincing and prancing, and
quite civil and polite: and they said they would
soon have a splendid feast ready, for they had
been killing rabbits and chickens all day, and
had not eaten them yet.

But now Jack felt a little difficulty; for he
knew it was the custom of the foxes to eat their
food raw, and he mentioned to them very politely
that, however pleasant that might be to a fox's

palate, he feared it would not agree with boys and girls.

"O, never fear about that," said the Queen Fox, who was wonderfully polite to Jack; "I've got a lazy slave inside the cave whom I generally employ in nursing the babies and tickling our tails when we want to go to sleep, and he knows all about cooking food for boys and girls."

So she and some other lady foxes went in to set this slave to work, and to mind the babies while he was cooking; and they soon returned bringing a grand feast, part of it nicely cooked for the little boys and girls, and the rest raw for the fox party. And they all set to; the foxes all sitting on their bushy tails, and even the most delicate Miss Foxes making no more bones at tearing a raw chicken to pieces with their teeth than you or I should at eating gingerbread.

After dinner Jack stood up, and said he was much obliged to all the foxes for their help and their kindness, and especially to his Majesty the King for his valuable services, and to her Majesty the Queen for this splendid feast: but, before he went, he should be so glad to see the whole family; could he be favoured with the sight of all the baby foxes?

"O, yes," said the Queen; "go, my dear (speaking to a young lady fox beside her), and make that lazy Tim bring out the babies; and mind you bite him if he does not handle them carefully."

At hearing the name of Tim, Jack pricked up his ears; and oh! how surprised he was when he saw his very brother Tim, who used to bully him so, and give himself such airs, come out quite woe-begone and crest-fallen, with a lot of baby foxes in his arms. And the little beasts were so cross and vicious, and when Tim tried to stroke and coax them, and said, " There, there, by-by, poor little foxy!" they only bit his fingers. But he dared not cry out, for fear of the Miss Fox, who was close by at his heels. When Tim saw his brother Jack, he was quite ashamed; but Jack went up to him quite heartily and kindly, and told him how he had found Toddles, and how they would all go home merrily together; for he was sure the foxes would let him go. They did not like the idea of parting with him at first; but, as Jack requested it, they were obliged to submit. And they were the more content, when the green-eyed dwarf said he should not mind staying with them instead of Tim; for he was tired of living alone in the wood, and thought he could stick up for himself. Then the rest, bidding good-bye to the foxes, Tim and Toddles, and the whole party of little boys and girls, set off on foot, accompanied by the hare. When they came to where Mother Lovechild lived, they saw nothing but the bare rock. But on Jack's striking it three times with the stick she had given him, it flew open; and inside they found the good old lady sitting at the head of the supper-table, and all the nice little girls laughing and eating away. And they were all so glad to see Jack again, who introduced to them his brother and sister, and all the other little boys and girls, and the hare. And the old lady said they were all welcome; and somehow the table grew ever so much larger, so that there was room for them all to sit down. So they all had supper together, and were as merry as grigs. After supper the old lady got up, and took off her spectacles to make a speech.

She said, "This is a very happy day for us all. I thought my friend Jack would succeed; for I saw he was a brave boy, when he was so kind to the little old woman who seemed in distress. And now, ladies and gentlemen, I will give you a toast: Long life and happiness to Jack Valiant!"

And then all the little boys and girls chirped in their pleasant little voices, "Here's your health, Jack Valiant."

And ever after that he was called Jack Valiant, instead of simple Jack. Tim was afraid all the time that she would say something unpleasant about him; but she was too kind and polite to do that. But she went on and said, "All the nice little girls that have been living with me I am going to send back to their parents to-morrow; and the other little boys and girls can stay with me for a while till I find out where they come from, and can send them back too, unless Jack Valiant likes to take one of them to be his little wife, when they are old enough to marry. I shall be glad, too, if the hare will stay with me, and also Tim, whom I will send home, when he is quite a good boy."

Then the hare and Tim, and all the other little girls and boys, said they would be very glad to stay with the old lady for a time; and Jack said he would like to take the little girl in the blue frock, who had helped him to find Toddles. And so it was all arranged. Jack and the little girl in the blue frock went home together, and in due time they were man and wife. And after a time Tim and the hare came home too. And the hare was changed into a girl; for she had been enchanted: not nearly so pretty as Jack's little girl, but still well enough; and Tim, who had now learnt to give up bragging and to be a good boy, married her. And Mother Lovechild came to their weddings, and was godmother to their children, and sent them presents on their birthdays; and I daresay she is living where she did to this very day.

THE CONCEITED PRINCESS.

HERE was once a Princess who was very conceited indeed. There was no bearing her, she was so conceited. And I'm afraid the Queen her mamma made her worse; for, whenever the King said, "What a pity it is our daughter is so conceited!" the Queen used to say, " Well, and hasn't she good reason to be conceited? Isn't she a Princess, and hasn't she a new dress every day worth £100, and isn't she remarkably good-looking, and very clever? If she mayn't be conceited, I wonder who may."

Now this was very foolish of the Queen: for, though what she said about the Princess's dress, and good looks, and cleverness, was true, yet it was not true that she had a right to be conceited. And it was not only wrong of her to be so, but also foolish. For her grand dresses would have sat on her much more gracefully, if she had not twisted and jerked herself about so in her conceit; and she would have looked much prettier than she did, if she had not simpered so, and made such grimaces; and people would have thought her much cleverer, if she had not given herself such airs about it; for very clever people are never conceited.

I'll tell you some things she did, she was so conceited. Sometimes she would stand looking at herself in a large looking-glass all day, smiling and smirking, and putting herself into all kinds of shapes, which she thought looked nice, but which were really very ridiculous. One day she broke the large looking-glass all to pieces, because she thought it did not do her justice. Then she was so conceited about her dresses. If the dressmaker brought her one that did not fit her exactly, or that she thought did not become her, she would tear it to pieces, and have the dressmaker put into prison. Then she was so conceited about her singing. She would have sung very well, if she had sung simply and naturally, without so many twirls and grimaces; but she could not bear to think that any one sung so well as herself. One day a famous singer came to court who sang beautifully, so that everybody admired him. She was angry at this; so she sat down to the piano, and sang herself, more conceitedly than ever; and because people did not seem to admire her so much as they had done the famous singer, she went to bed crying, and next morning got the Queen to send the famous singer to prison. The courtiers got quite sick of her airs and graces, but, as the Queen backed her up, they were obliged to pretend they thought her better dressed, and handsomer, and cleverer, than anybody else : and this flattery made her worse. And so this poor Princess, who, if she had not been conceited, would have been a very nice girl, became a bore to everybody, and everybody laughed at her in their hearts. The worst of it was, that nobody would marry her, she was so conceited. Many Princes come to her father's court, intending to ask her to marry them, having heard the fame of her beauty and accomplishments ; but, when they had seen her for a day or two, they all went away, saying that they could not do with a wife that was so conceited.

At last the King of Peacocks came to her father's court, desiring to marry her. He was terribly conceited himself; as conceited as she was. He was dressed in peacock's feathers, and carried a train like a huge peacock's tail, which he spread in the air as he walked, strutting and pluming himself, and expecting everybody to admire him. He was so conceited himself, that he took no notice of her conceit ; for he thought of nobody but himself. So he was quite ready to marry her, and, though he was hot the kind of person that the King and Queen would have wished for some time ago, yet they were so tired of having the Princess on their hands, and so vexed that no one else would take her, that they gave their consent. As for her, she thought the King of the Peacocks a very fine fellow, and her own conceit prevented her from perceiving his conceit, as his conceit prevented him from perceiving her's.

Now there was a young page about the court, who was very fond of the Princess. He was the son of one of the King's shepherds, who had been taken into the palace to help the cook, when a little boy, and he had behaved so well that he had got promoted to be one of the twenty pages that waited on the twenty ladies that waited on the Princess. She never took the least notice of him, and hardly knew that there was such a person. But he admired her exceedingly, and thought her the most beautiful Princess that had ever lived; and when the other pages used to laugh at her among themselves, and call her an odious conceited minx, he used to be angry, and say that he would not hear a word against her. He was constantly looking at her, though he did not venture to let her see that he was doing so;

and he thought it a great happiness if he could pick up a glove' or' a handkerchief that she had dropped, and present it to the lady whose duty it was to present it to the Princess. So, when it was arranged that she should marry the King of the Peacocks, he plucked up his courage, and requested the Queen that he might be allowed to go with the Princess among her train-bearers. The Queen at first seemed astonished at his presumption; and the Princess who was sitting by the Queen in an arm-chair, looking at herself in a small looking-glass that she carried in her hand, cast a look on him of unutterable scorn. But he pressed his request so earnestly, and was so respectful, and spoke so prettily, and looked so handsome all the time, that his request was granted.

At last, when all was settled about the marriage, the King of the Peacocks went away to his own kingdom, to make things ready for his new Queen; and it was arranged that she should follow him with Prince Kangaroo, her brother, and a large train of lords and ladies, in a month's time. When the month was past they all set out in great state, and the page, whose name was Sunny-face, followed as one of the Princess's train-bearers. He had not much to do on the journey, as she rode in a coach, and did not require any one to bear her train, except when she got out in the evening, when her twelve train-bearers had to carry her train, which was six yards long, and spread it out behind her grace-fully, when she sat down to supper; and they had to carry it again when she walked to the coach in the morning, and fold it elegantly round the necks of the ladies who sat in the coach with her. During the day, all Sunny-face had to do was to run behind the coach with the rest, and pick up anything that might be dropped. It was a long and tiring journey, over mountains and valleys, through forests and wide plains.

One night they stopped in a beautiful valley; and, when the Princess had supped and gone to bed, Sunny-face took a walk by moonlight along the clear river that ran through the valley. As he was walking, he met the nymph of the river; for in that country rivers had a sort of fairies, called water-nymphs, that lived in them, one at least in each, and who were so much a part of the river they lived in that, if they left it, the river would dry up, and if the river dried up, the nymph would die. If the river was clear and bright, the people of that country knew it was because the nymph was in good spirits; if it was fuller of water than usual, they knew that she had been weeping; if it ever got very shallow

and scant of water, they knew that she was lan-
guishing and ill.

That night the river, by which Sunny-face was
walking, was very bright and sparkling, which
was a sign that its nymph was in a particularly
good humour. She was in such a good humour,
that she had come out of the stream to take a
walk on the banks, and Sunny-face met her. She
was very beautiful, and was dressed in a green
robe that clung round her like the leaves and
grasses that grow in rivers, and she had a wreath
of water lilies round her head. Her voice was
very sweet, and like the sound of a pleasant gurgling stream, as she spoke to him and said,
"Well, Master Sunny-face, so you are in love with
the conceited Princess, are you? You'd better
give it up, for you'll find her very hard to please."

"Madam," he replied, "I cannot approve of
your calling my Princess conceited; and if you
had better manners, you would not have hurt my
feelings by using such a word. I am her servant,
and it is not for me to find fault with anything she
does, or to allow anyone else to call her names."

"Oh!" said the nymph; "but I know her
well enough; and I can assure you that, however
faithfully you serve her, she never wastes a
thought on you, and you'll do yourself no good
by remaining in her service. Wouldn't it be far

nicer for you to leave her, and come and live in
the river with me? I could change you into a
water-sprite in a moment; and we could play together for ever in this pleasant stream, and be as
happy as the day is long."

"Madam," he replied, still very polite, "I feel
much obliged to you for your very kind proposal;
but you must allow me to say that nothing could
tempt me to leave the service of my mistress, as
long as she allows me to follow her; and, whether
she ever notices me or not, I shall have the satis-
faction of feeling that I have done my duty."

"Well," replied the nymph, still in a good
humour, "a wilful lad must have his way. It is
not very polite of you to take my condescending
offer in the way you have done; but, at any rate,
I admire your loyalty, and will be your friend.
Do you desire to do your Princess a service?"

"Of course I do," said he.

"Well, then," she replied; "let me tell you
that great trouble and danger await her. I know
the King of the Peacocks well enough; for my
river flows through his kingdom many miles from
hence; and he is the most intolerable coxcomb
that ever lived, and has neither brains nor heart.
If your Princess marries him she will be miserable
for life: they'll both be so conceited together
that they'll quarrel continually; and, as he will

have all the power, he will soon neglect her, and then be cruel to her, and perhaps in the end send some of his peacocks to peck her eyes out. If you'll do what I tell you, you may save her from such a sad fate; but don't expect that she'll ever care for you, whatever you do for her; she'll probably scorn you all the same. Are you willing to save her with this prospect, or will you be a wise boy, and leave her to her fate, and stay with me?"

"I desire", said Sunny-face, "nothing but to do all I can to serve my Princess."

"Well, then," said the nymph, "before she arrives at the King of the Peacocks' kingdom, manage by all means in your power to get to speak to her, and implore her, as she values her happiness, to dress herself in a plain print or muslin frock, and to wear no jewels, when the King comes to meet her. Tell her you have been informed by a powerful fairy that this is necessary in order to avoid a terrible misfortune. If she does as you desire her, the King of the Peacocks will be so offended at her meeting him plainly dressed—though really her dress will be in the best taste—that he will cock his plumes in the air, and go home and break off the match. And so the Princess will be saved. If she should refuse after all to do as you desire her, the only

way of saving her is this : As she walks from her
coach to meet the King, run forward as they are
bowing and curtseying to each other, and throw
the water out of this bottle into her face. And
now good-bye; I may possibly see you again. I
must now return to my stream, which is begin-
ning already to dry up because I am out of it."

. With that she gave him a crystal bottle, and
glided into the river, which at once began to
flow fuller and brighter than before. /

It was many days before Sunny-face could succeed in getting to speak to the Princess. He
often was on the point of trying, but she bridled
herself up so, and looked so scornful and proud,
that his heart always failed him. So he told his
secret to one of the ladies-in-waiting, who had
always been kind to him; and she promised to do
what she could to get him a chance of speaking.
She managed it at last. It was the last evening
of the journey; and next day they expected to
meet the King. The Princess was lolling on a
couch in her silk dress embroidered with gold,
smiling into her hand-mirror, and having all the
grand dresses and jewels spread out before her
that she thought of wearing next day. It seemed
impossible to decide which she should wear; and
when she had got very cross about it, and was in
a complete state of perplexity, the lady who was

H

Sunny-face's friend, said, " May it please your
Royal Highness, I think I shall be able to help
you to a decision on this very important subject.
So great is the fame of your Royal Highness's
perfections that even the Powers of the air and
water take an interest in you. And I am assured
by one of your attendants that a powerful water-
nymph has appeared to him for the sole purpose
of pointing out the costume which will set off
your charms to the best advantage."

The Princess was pleased at hearing this, and
commanded the attendant spoken of to be brought
before her. She looked surprised when so humble a person as Sunny-face appeared, and looked
down on him with a look that seemed to say, " I
wonder what an absurd insignificant little varlet
like this can have the impertinence to say about
it ?"

However, she allowed him to speak, which he
did very respectfully, but earnestly; repeating all
the water-nymph had told him to say. The lady
then joined in, saying, " The very thing of all
others ! You are yourself, Madam, so simple
and unaffected, that a simple costume will be in
admirable keeping. Besides, the taste of a true
Princess will be shown in your contempt of outside ornament, which inferior people make such
a point of; and it will appear how little your

royal grace depends upon what you wear. Allow me to suggest: in a simple dress of white
muslin, exquisitely fitting, with narrow blue rib-
bon round the throat, and a blue belt round the
waist, a lovely little plain straw bonnet with
simple blue trimmings and strings, and pale
primrose gloves, you will look perfectly ravish-
ing, and the King of the Peacocks will be enchanted."

The lady would have gone on much longer,
for she had a glib tongue, had not the Princess,
who had been bridling herself up more and more,
and getting angrier and angrier, at last thrown
the looking-glass at her head, and exclaimed, "A
pretty idea, that I should go to meet the King,
who will be grandeur itself, dressed like a mere
peasant girl! It 's all a lie about the water-
nymph; and, if not, the water-nymph 's a fool.
As if I hadn't better taste than any water-nymph.
And as for that absurd and impertinent page, let
him be taken out and soundly whipped; and let
me never see his face again."

So poor Sunny-face was taken out and whipped
for his pains, and told that he must carry the
Princess's train no more, nor come within sight
of her, if he valued his life. He did not care
half so much for the whipping as for being turned
off from being the Princess's train-bearer; and

he cared still more for her not having taken the advice of the water-nymph. But, come what might, he resolved to save her, if he could. So, next day, when Prince Kangaroo, her brother, handed her from her coach, and led her by the hand to meet the King of the Peacocks, Sunny-face lurked behind the trees, where he could not be seen, to watch his opportunity.

The Princess's dress was something quite alarming. In her conceit she had gone to the opposite extreme to what had been advised her, and had all the colours of the rainbow about her. On her head she had a live peacock with his tail spread, in honour of the King of the Peacocks, the poor bird being tied fast, so that he could not move his legs, but only his head and his tail; and he had a necklace of diamonds round his neck. As for the Princess herself, she was so laden with jewels that she could hardly walk ; and her scarlet satin train was double its usual length, twelve yards long, and so heavy with gold that the twenty-four train-bearers could hardly carry it. And two lords with large looking-glasses walked on each side of her, holding them so that she could see herself, whichever way she looked: and she simpered, and minced, and twisted herself, to an extent that was quite astonishing.

Sunny-face did not like to see all this, and

thought that she would have looked much better
in a plain white muslin dress; and in his heart
he could not help thinking what a pity it was she
was so conceited. But he felt convinced all the
time that she was a good girl at bottom, only she
had been flattered and spoilt, and that she would
turn out everything that could be wished in the
end. Besides, he said to himself, She is my mistress, and it is not my place to find fault with
her.

Well, by-and-by, the King of the Peacocks
met her, as grand as she was; and they stood for
some time bowing and curtseying in a manner
that was wonderful.

All at once Sunny-face rushed forward from his
hiding-place, knocking the courtiers down in his
haste, took the cork out of the crystal bottle, and
threw the water in the face of the Princess. What
was his dismay to see that, as soon as he had done
so, her face became as black as a coal, her silks
and satin turned to canvass, her jewels to common
stones, her gold to lead, and the peacock on her
head to a toad! The King of the Peacocks, who
was just on the point of taking her hand when
this happened, set up a loud shriek, such as peacocks utter, turned round in a most ruffled condition, and retreated home with his feathers in
the air, crying, "Squaw, squaw".

Prince Kangaroo rushed at Sunny-face with his sword drawn, to kill him, and others followed also for the same purpose : but Sunny-face, who was very active, ran quickly through the trees till he came to the river, into which he plunged for safety, and sank, and was seen no more. They thought he was certainly drowned, and returned to the Princess, whom they found in the most dreadful hysterics. As they were trying to bring her round with cold water and smelling salts, they saw the army of the Peacocks coming to avenge the insult that had been offered to His Majesty, and away they had to go helter-skelter.

Nearly all the attendants of the Princess thought only of their own safety, for they cared nothing for her, seized on the horses and carriages, and escaped to their own country, though many of them were lost on the way. Prince Kangaroo alone turned to fight the Peacock army, and was taken prisoner. The Princess was carried off through the trees by the lady who had been so kind to Sunny-face, and who was the only person who stuck to her; and at last they managed to escape pursuit, and took refuge in a dark cave, which was hidden by shrubs and creepers. And there they had to live, supporting themselves on the berries that grew near, the Princess still giving herself airs, and not bearing to believe that she had lost all her beauty and grand ornaments, and expecting the lady to admire and humour her; but, whenever she caught sight of her own face and figure in the looking-glass which she still had hanging to her waist, she uttered loud shrieks, and went into hysterics. At last, one day, being able to bear it no longer, she took the glass and dashed it to pieces; and after this she felt much happier. And by degrees hunger and hardship and loneliness had a wonderfully good effect upon her, and she began to feel how foolish and conceited she had been, and was very sorry for it; and she begged the lady to forgive all her former humours and absurdities; and the lady liked her much better, and found her much pleasanter to wait on, black and shabby as she was, than she had done when she was grand and beautiful. And so they lived a long time in this cave, till one day, to their surprise, on looking out, they saw a dish of delicately cooked fish placed before it, which they took in, and enjoyed exceedingly. Another day they found ·a bottle of excellent wine; and every day they found something; sometimes food; sometimes articles of clothing, plain but very good and comfortable; sometimes blankets and bedding; so that by-and-by they found their cave quite a comfortable place to live in. They were very anxious to find out who brought them all these nice things; but for a long time they could get sight of nobody. At last, as they were peeping out very early in the morning, they spied a handsome young man escaping from the mouth of the cave, where he had just left something. They called loudly after him, so that he turned and looked; and, when they made earnest signs to him, he came towards them timidly. The lady knew at once that it was Sunny-face; but the Princess had taken so little notice of him when she was grand and conceited, that she did not know him again. But now she thought him remarkably handsome, and said to herself—"O that I were not so black and ugly! How much nicer it would be to marry this young man than the King of the Peacocks!"

He approached them with great respect, and, kneeling before the Princess, acknowledged that it was he who had supplied them with food and clothing, through the help (he said) of a kind friend, and hoped that he had made her Royal Highness more comfortable than before. She insisted on his rising from his knees, and thanked him in the most simple and cordial way; and it was delightful to see how nicely he behaved, treating her with quite as much respect as if she had been beautiful and adorned with jewels.

After that he came and talked to them every day,
always bringing something nice; but, when the
Princess begged him to tell her who he was, and
where he came from, he always said that he was
not allowed to do so; and the lady, seeing that it
was to be a secret, did not tell her mistress what
she knew about him. After a time he asked
them one evening to be so kind as to walk with him
along the river, and they would learn something
about him. They were afraid at first of leaving
the cave, for fear some of the Peacock people
might surprise them; but he assured them there
was no danger; so they went with him. When
they had come to a secluded place, beside a pool
in the river overhung with willows, the Nymph
of the river appeared before them. She spoke
in her soft gurgling voice, and said—" Princess,
I trust you are cured at last of your intolerable
conceit, which used to make you odious. In
this belief, I beg to inform you that this is your
former page and trainbearer, Sunny-face, whom
you used to scorn, and whom you once treated
so shamefully, when he gave you good advice.
Supposing that now he were to make you an
offer of marriage, I presume that you would not
reject it." The nymph spoke scornfully; but
the Princess took it in good part, and said that
she was ashamed to confess that she had formerly

taken so little notice of her faithful page that she had not known him again; but that she remembered him now; that she was very sorry for all her bad treatment of him; but that, as to his making her an offer of marriage, she knew that was out of the question, as no one would take a poor black ugly princess like herself.

The nymph then turned to Sunny-face, and said—"You hear what she says: what do *you* say?" He replied that, as to any change in the Princess's appearance, that made no change in his devotion to her; but, as for offering her marriage, that was a piece of presumption he could not have dreamt of, had not the nymph mentioned it; and that all he hoped for was that the Princess would forgive his having offended her formerly, and take him into her service as before. "Hurrah!" said the water-nymph. "These are very pretty speeches, to be sure! Things seem at last to be in the proper train: let me see if I can throw a little more light on the matter." With that she took some water in the palm of her hand, and threw it in the Princess's face; when all at once she had her former complexion again, and stood as beautiful as ever, and dressed in the very dress that the lady had recommended her to wear on the day she was to meet the King of the Peacocks. "And now," said the nymph, " all is settled in this quarter. No more fine speeches to each other; for of course you are to be married : and I can assure you, Princess, that Sunny-face has deserved all the kindness and affection you can shew him; and I assure you, too, Sunny-face, that your Princess has not now an atom of conceit left in her, and she will make you an excellent wife. And now" (she continued) "it is time we thought of Prince Kangaroo, who has been all this time a prisoner in the King of the Peacocks' palace. Stand you on the hill yonder, and you will see what I will do." She then glided into the water, and they stood on the neighbouring hill to watch what would happen. As they looked, the river began to rise, and at last filled all the valley in a tremendous torrent. It swept round to the other side of the hill on which they stood, and, though they could not see what it did there, they soon saw the results. For the flood came rushing again round the hill on the other side, bringing with it beams and furniture out of the King of the Peacocks' palace, which it had swept away; and by-and-by, struggling among the water, the King himself and all his courtiers, with their peacocks' plumes sadly drenched and draggled : and they were all soon swept away out of sight into the sea, crying " Dear me !" and " Squaw, Squaw !"

After this there appeared in a boat Prince Kangaroo, floating along quietly and safely; and, when he had come near them, the water went down, and he stood safe and sound on the hill beside them. The river now flowed within its banks as usual, and the nymph again appeared before them, waving her arms in the air, and sprinkling water. The water which she sprinkled formed itself into a coach drawn by flying fishes, which she said was intended to convey Prince Kangaroo back to his own country, and anyone else he liked to take with him. He said at once that, if the lady who had been so faithful and kind to his sister in her distress, would go with him and be his wife, he should be exceedingly happy. And she consented without much ado. So away they went in the flying chariot. As for Sunny-face and the Princess, they remained where they were, and became King and Queen of the kingdom of the Peacocks.

THE TALKING FISH.

ID you ever hear of a talking fish? Well, I'll tell you about one. I'm going to tell you a wonderful story: I hope you'll believe it.

Near Rummyhole Hall, in the county of Rummyshire, there was a river called the river Silvery. Mr. and Mrs. Rumfolk lived in Rummyhole Hall, and they had a little boy called Funny, and a little girl called Queer. Funny and Queer used to go and fish in the river Silvery with an old whip-handle belonging to Mr. Rumfolk for a rod, and some silk thread that Queer got out of Mrs. Rumfolk's workbox for a line, and a crooked pin for a hook; and they baited the hook with bits of meat that they put in their pockets at dinner-time. One day, as they were fishing, a great fish bit at the hook; but he was so strong, that they could not pull him out of the water. They got him pulled to the top of the water, and saw that he had a golden head and a silver body; but, before

they could get him pulled to the shore, he
jumped off the hook, and away he went down
into the water again. The next day they hooked
him again, but he got away just as before. The
third day they hooked him again; and, just as
they had managed to pull him to the top of the
water, Funny gave a sudden jerk to the rod,
and jerked him out of the water on to the shore.
And there he lay gasping for a time, and opened
his mouth, as if he wanted to talk. But he
could not get his voice, till Queer went and
tickled him under the throat; and then he said,
in a gasping husky sort of way, " Put me into
the water again." " O yes, very likely," said
Funny, " when we've had such trouble to get
you out! We'll take you home, and have you
fried for our supper." And Queer said, "We'll
make ornaments of your gold and silver scales."
" No, you won't," said the fish: "you'll just put
my body into the water again; you can hold me
by the head, if you like, so that I can't get
away; and I'll tell you something very curious.
I can't talk comfortably on the land." So they
put his body into the water, and held him by the
head, so that he could not get away. And what
do you think he did? He began to sing. I'll
tell you what he sang; and he sang it to a very

pretty tune, which I am sorry I cannot remember. He sang as follows :—

> " Little people, Funny and Queer,
> Listen well to what I say ;
> Do not squeeze my head, my dear,
> I'm not going to swim away.

> " I'm the King of all the Fishes—
> Bother ! do not squeeze me so—
> I can grant you all your wishes,
> If you'll only let me go.

> " Only mention what you wish ;
> If you let me get away,
> On the word of a royal fish,
> You shall have it all to-day."

When Funny heard this, he told the fish he should like an apple pie to be under his pillow every night when he went to bed; and Queer said she would like a pair of new kid gloves to be on her dressing-table every morning when she got up. For Funny was very fond of apple pie, and Queer was very fond of nice kid gloves, which she had only just begun to wear. And the fish said they should have what they wished, if they would let him go. So they let him go, and went home. And, sure enough, when Funny went to bed, he found an apple pie under his pillow; and, when the nurse had gone to bed, and all was quiet, he woke up Queer, and they ate it together, and enjoyed it very much. And,

sure enough, when Queer got up in the morning,
she found a pair of new kid gloves on her table,
which she put on directly, and called Funny to
see how nice they looked. And this happened
every night and every morning; and the nurse
wondered why it was that they had so little
appetite for breakfast; for she did not know of
the apple pie that they ate every night in bed;
and Mrs. Rumfolk wondered how it was that
Queer always kept her gloves so clean and nice;
for she did not know that she had a new pair
every day.

After a time the two children began to be dis-
satisfied with what they had got, and thought
they would like something else from the King
of the Fishes. So Queer put on her new kid
gloves, and Funny crammed the remains of his
apple pie into his pocket, to munch by the way;
and they went to the river Silvery with their
rod and line and crooked pin, which they baited
this time with a bit of apple pie. Just as they
had thrown it into the water, the fish put his
head up, and began to sing as follows to a very
pretty tune :—

> " Little people, Funny and Queer,
>   You may tell me what your wish is ;
>   But you shall not catch again
>   Me the King of all the Fishes.

"Take away that nasty pin—
How it hurt the other day !—
But I'll give you all you want,
Since you let me swim away."

Then Funny told the fish that it was of no use
having apple pie to eat, when he had his Latin
exercise to do, and that he wanted to have his
exercise done for him. And Queer said that it
was of no use having such nice gloves, when she
had her sewing to do; for she might not wear
them then, and the needle pricked her fingers
and made them sore; so she wanted her sewing
to be all done for her. And the fish said it
should all be done for them. Then he dived
down into the water, and soon came up again
with two gold rings in his mouth, which he gave
to Funny and Queer, and told them that, whenever they wanted anything, they should throw
the rings into the water, and say—

"Pretty Gold and Silver Fish,
Come and give us what we wish;"

and he would come up, and give them anything
they asked for that was not unreasonable. So
they went home; and, sure enough, every morning Funny found his Latin exercise all done for
him when he got up; and Queer found her sewing all finished beautifully. And Mr. and Mrs.
Rumfolk were quite pleased with their children;

I

for they thought they had done it all themselves. So they let them go out quite early in the morning to play; and they went into the woods, Queer with her kid gloves on, and Funny with an apple pie in his pocket, and they used to enjoy themselves very much. Now as these children grew bigger they were very fond of reading Fairy Tales. And they read there so much about Kings and Queens, and Fairy Princes, and Fairy Princesses, that they thought they should like to be a King and Queen themselves: and Funny thought he would like to marry a Fairy Princess, and Queer thought she would like a Fairy Prince to come and ask her to be his wife. So, when they were playing in the wood, they used to pretend they were a King and Queen; and Queer made two crowns of gold paper, which they wore on their heads, and used to get her Mama's parasol, which she pretended was a sceptre; and Funny used to pretend with his Papa's walking-stick. And Funny dressed up the cat, and pretended she was his Fairy Princess; and Queer dressed up the little dog, and pretended it was her Fairy Prince. At last they got tired of pretending, and wanted to be a real King and Queen, and to sit on real golden thrones, and wear real crowns, and carry real sceptres, and to have nothing else to do, and to have as much money as they wanted, and to have a lot of subjects under them, and to be able to cut as many people's heads off as they liked, and to have a real Fairy Prince, and a real Fairy Princess to come and marry them. So they went to the river Silvery, and threw their two gold rings in, and said—

> " Pretty Gold and Silver Fish,
> Come and give us what we wish."

And the fish popped his head up, with the two rings in his mouth, and asked them what they wanted. So they told him. He did not answer at first, but seemed to be thinking. At last he sang :—

> " Little people, Funny and Queer,
>   I told you to ask for something reasonable ;
> But really this request, my dear,
>   From little folks is quite unseasonable.

> " But if you'll wait another year,
>   And be a very good girl and boy,
> Attend to all the words you hear,
>   And never break a single toy ;

> " If Queer herself her work will do,
>   And if she can't will say ' I'll try ;'
> And Funny learn his lessons too,
>   Nor care so much for apple pie ;

> " Then come again to Silvery river,
>   And what will happen you shall see ;
> An idle boy or girl can never
>   Be made a King and Queen by me."

Funny and Queer could not understand why it should be necessary for a King to know Latin, or for a Queen to be able to sew; for they thought they would have nothing to do but sit on their thrones. But, as the fish had dived down again, and would say no more, there was no help for it but to do as he had told them. So they went home again; and after that Funny never found his exercise done for him, nor Queer her sewing finished, when they got up in the morning. So they had to try to do what they could themselves; and they tried very hard, and succeeded very well, so that Mr. and Mrs. Rumfolk were still much pleased with them. And Funny used to find only half an apple pie under his pillow in the morning, and that only once a week; but he found this was much better for him, as he used to eat too much before, till he felt quite sick. And Queer only found a pair of kid gloves on her table once a month now, instead of every morning; and this was much better for her too, as she had to take more care of them; and she did take so much care of them that Mrs. Rumfolk never found out the difference. And from all this it appears that it is not all the little boys and girls who get all they want, but those who take care of what is given them, and are thankful for it, and who always try to be good, and to do their work and lessons well, that are really the happiest.

Well, when a year was over, they went again to the river Silvery, and threw their two gold rings in, and said—

> " Pretty Gold and Silver Fish,
>   Come and give us what we wish."

And the fish popped his head up, and asked them what they wanted. So they said that they had done all that he had told them, and that they wanted him to make them a King and Queen. Then the fish sang :—

> " Little people, Funny and Queer,
>   What you ask's no easy thing ;
> But you've been so good this year,
>   You shall be a Queen and King.
>
> " Make a little paper boat,
>   Filled with little paper men ;
> Let it on the water float,
>   Shut your eyes and look again."

So they made a beautiful little boat of gold paper, and cut out little men of blue paper, and put them in; and they put it on the river and shut their eyes. And, when they opened them again, it was turned into a real boat glittering like gold, and with sailors in it with blue jackets and trousers, who rowed it to the shore, that Funny and Queer might get into it; and the fish popped his head up and sang :—

" Get into the boat, my dears,
    The prettiest boat that e'er was seen ;
. Little folks must feel no fears,
    Who would be a King and Queen."

So they got in, though they were rather afraid ;
and, as soon as they were in, it floated away down
the river so quick that they could hardly see ; and
the fish swam before them all the time, with his
golden head above the water, singing beautifully.
When they had floated a long long way, the river
grew broader, till it became like a great lake ;
and then the boat stopped, and the fish before
them sang out in a loud musical voice,—

" Down, down, to the coral halls
    Where the tuneful mermaids sing ;
Down, down, to the pearly walls
    Of the palace of the King."

Suddenly there was a great wind, and a great
whirlpool in the water ; and the boat went round
and round, and down and down, to the bottom of
the lake, and Funny and Queer found themselves
out of breath and frightened in a beautiful palace
under the water, built of coral and shining with
pearls, in which were two thrones of mother of
pearl ; and a merman and a mermaid led them to
the thrones, and directed them to sit upon them,
and put two crowns on their heads, and sceptres
in their hands. And their old friend the fish was

now changed into a merman ; that is, his head
and the upper part of his body were now those of
a beautiful young man, but the lower part was
that of a fish still, with silver scales. And he
introduced to them a mermaid, the lower part of
whose body was also that of a fish, but the upper
part that of a beautiful young lady ; and he said
that this was his sister, and that he and she were
King and Queen of all the Fishes, but that they
had given up their thrones to Funny and Queer
because he had promised they should be a King
and Queen. So they were a King and Queen at
last, and sat all day on their thrones with their
crowns on, the mermen and mermaids singing
beautifully to them all the time. But they did
not enjoy it much, and thought it had been much
pleasanter when they had only played at being
King and Queen in the wood.

When they were getting very much tired of it,
their old friend the fish, who was now a merman,
asked Queer if she would be his wife, and asked
Funny if he would marry the mermaid, his sister,
and then they would be all Kings and Queens
together. But Funny and Queer did not like to
marry people who had fishes' tails, and for a long
time they said no. But at last, as they were tired
of sitting on their thrones doing nothing, and as
the upper parts of the merman and mermaid were

very beautiful, and as they thought how kind they had been in giving up their thrones to them, they consented.

So they were married, Funny to the mermaid, and Queer to the merman; and there was a very grand wedding. When they woke next morning, everything was changed. They were no longer under the water, but in a beautiful palace in a beautiful country, with trees growing round them. And the merman and mermaid had become a beautiful Prince and Princess from top to toe.

And the Prince told them that he and his sister had been enchanted, and obliged to live under the water, as a merman and mermaid when they were at the bottom, and as fishes with silver bodies and golden heads when they came to the top; and that there had been nothing that could break their enchantment but a good little boy and a good little girl marrying them as they were; and that he had contrived all that had happened on purpose; he had let himself be caught at first in Silvery river on purpose, and had made everything happen just as it did.

So Funny and Queer were very happy, and, now that they were on dry land, and could go about where they liked, they enjoyed being a real King and Queen very much indeed; and they liked it all the better because Funny's wife and

Queer's husband had once been enchanted in the form of fishes; for this made it more like what they had read of in their fairy tales. And they soon sent to Rummyhole Hall in the county of Rummy-shire, for their papa and mama, Mr. and Mrs. Rumfolk, who came to live with them, and were quite pleased to find their children so grand as a King and a Queen.

And they lived very happily together all the rest of their lives.

I N a very distant land, beyond the Carrowibbeway Mountains, there lived once a King and Queen, who were the richest King and Queen in the world. They grew so rich at last, that gold became as common a thing with them as stones are with other people; and this made them very proud. One thing they wanted, however, that no gold could buy; and that was a child. At last they got one, and they were so delighted that they didn't know what to do. It was a little girl, with blue eyes, and flaxen hair, and a beautiful complexion like blancmange and strawberries, and everybody said there had never been so pretty a child before. So, to show how pleased they were, they passed a law that henceforth nothing should be used in the palace, not even the door-mats and the washing-tubs, but what was made of gold; and they called the child's name " Little Goldina." She grew up with nothing but gold about her. She played with little golden dolls, and ate her meals off golden plates with a golden spoon and fork ; and, though she could not eat gold, yet all she ate was gilt all over before it was brought to table ; and she wore dresses woven of beautifully fine gold thread ; and she learnt to write on golden slates with a little golden pencil, and learnt to read out of golden books ; and, when she was naughty (which she very seldom was), the Queen whipt her with a little golden rod. But she had rather not have been whipt at all, though her governess told her it was a very grand thing to be whipt by a Queen with a rod of gold.

Well, nothing is quite perfect in this world ; and, as Goldina did not quite like the rod, though it was of gold, so there came something by and by that the King and Queen did not like. For, from seeing nothing but gold, and smelling nothing but gold, and handling nothing but gold, and tasting gold in all their food, everybody in the palace soon began to look like gold ; their skins grew golden-coloured, the bloom in their cheeks turned yellow ; and the ladies' hands, though they washed them continually in cream, and wore gloves night and day, would not keep white, as they used to do. At last they made the best of what they could not help, and said that a golden complexion was a beauty, and a sign of high rank : and so golden complexions became the fashion ;

and ladies who did not belong to the court, and
retained their natural colour, dyed their skins
yellow, in order to be in the fashion, and to look
like the ladies of the court. But, for all this, the
King and Queen did not like to see their little
daughter losing her beautiful complexion like
blancmange and strawberries, and getting to look
the colour of a guinea. Besides, her little skin
was not as soft as it used to be, but grew hard and
shiny like metal. The lords and ladies told them
that all this was just as it should be, and very
beautiful. But the King and Queen, though they
pretended to think so, did not really think so at
all, and used to cry to each other, when they
were alone.

One day the King said to the Queen, "My
dear!"—for, though they were so grand, they
called each other "my dear" when they were
quite alone—"My dear, this won't do! What's
to be done?"

"Throw all your gold into the sea," said the
Queen, "and then, perhaps, she'll come right
again."

"I couldn't do it," said the King, "for what
would my subjects say? And it might not do any
good after all." And then they both began to cry.

So the Queen proposed they should consult the
Hermit of the Dismal Cave, who was said to know

everything. So they set off at night, without anybody knowing, and travelled more than a hundred miles to find the Hermit of the Dismal Cave. He was an old man, quite blind, and with a white beard reaching to his feet, and he had lived a hundred years in that cave quite alone, eating nuts, and saying his prayers.

And they asked him what they were to do to keep little Goldina from turning entirely into gold.

And he said the King must melt his golden palace down, and throw all his golden things into the sea.

But the King asked if that would bring Goldina's complexion back again.

And the Hermit said that he could not be sure of that; but it would prevent her from getting any worse.

And the King said that he was very proud of all his gold, and could not give it up, unless doing so would quite recover Goldina.

So the Hermit said the King was a great donkey, and deserved no help; but, as Goldina was not to blame, he would tell him how he might cure her entirely. He must send her to the Island of the Crystal Mountains, where the hills were all made of glass; for if she lived there for three whole years she would get her complexion back again; but she must take care never to look at herself in the Glass Mountains, or something very bad would happen.

So the King and Queen went home again, and sent people in ships all round the world to find the Island of the Crystal Mountains. Only one of the ships came back, the captain of which said he had found the island, a very great way off, but that it was very hard to get to it, there were such storms and rocks to go through. But the King thought nothing of that, he was so anxious to get Goldina cured. So he had a very strong ship made, and he put in it very skilful sailors, and away it sailed with Goldina and her governess and her nurse on board, and a lot of clever masons to build her a palace to live in.

After many days they came to the Island of the Crystal Mountains. When they were many miles from it, they saw it glittering over the sea; and very beautiful it looked, with colours playing about it like those of a rainbow or a diamond. And, when they got there, the clever masons set to work and built a palace in no time, all of wood and stone, and with no gold in it at all; and, when it was finished, the ship sailed away, to return after three years, leaving there Goldina, her governess and nurse, and servants to wait on them.

For two whole years they lived there, Goldina doing her lesson with the governess, and walking out in the afternoon. And they never looked at themselves in the Glass Mountains all the time, though it was not easy to help doing so, when they were out walking. But the governess ordered a wall to be built at the side of the road next the mountains; and, as they could not see through a wall, it was easier to help looking at themselves.

When the two years were over, a ship came to the island, sent by the King to see how they were getting on. And, when the captain of the ship came to them, they almost burst out laughing to see him, he looked so queer, and hard, and shiny, and yellow. For they themselves had been getting to look all right again during these two years; only the change came so gradually that they had not observed it in each other, and they could not observe it in themselves, as they had never looked in a looking-glass (the King having given particular orders that there were to be no looking-glasses in the palace) any more than in the glass mountain. And so, when they saw the captain, he took them by surprise, and they had no idea that they had looked almost as bad themselves two years ago. The captain, on his part, was equally astonished at their appearance; and, though he had long said as others did, and almost persuaded himself that to look like gold was the

greatest beauty, yet, when he saw Goldina, with
her face almost like blanc-mange and strawberries again, he could not help exclaiming with ad-
miration and delight. Now it was a pity that he
did so; for so far neither Goldina, nor the governess, nor the nurse, had ever thought about
their looks; but now they all began to think
how beautiful they must be. And, when the
captain was gone, Goldina, who always said what
she thought, asked why they should not all take
just one peep at themselves in the glass mountains; but the governess scolded her for ever
thinking of such a thing, and told the nurse to
take her to bed directly. And the nurse, as she
put her to bed, scolded her too, and said she
must be a very vain child to think so much of
her appearance. But, as soon as she had put
her to bed, the nurse took her own bonnet and
shawl, and sneaked down stairs to have a look at
herself on the sly in the glass mountain. But
the governess was too much for her, for she was
waiting at the front door to watch the nurse;
and, when she saw what she was after, she gave
her a tremendous scolding, and sent her upstairs
to her room, and locked her in. But when she
had done so, she took her own bonnet and shawl,
and away she went to have just one peep at herself in the glass mountains. She was so pleased

with her own looks that she stayed there all
night, and only got back just in time to unlock
the nurse's door before the servants got up, and
go to bed herself as if she had been there all
night. But, as soon as the nurse heard her door
unlocked, off she started as fast as her legs could
carry her, to have a look at herself in the glass
mountain And, as soon as breakfast was over,
the governess went there too; and, when she
had gone, Goldina thought she might as well go
like the rest; and there they all stayed looking
at themselves all day, and thinking how beautiful they were. And the more they looked, the
more they wanted to look again; and so went day
after day, and no lessons were done; nothing
but look, look, look at themselves in the glass
mountains. Now, this was all very silly and
wrong of them: but, when people begin to be
vain of their looks, and to think much about
them, they grow very silly, and come to grief.

When another year was gone, the ship came
again to take them home; and they all went to
meet the captain, smiling and mincing, and thinking how much he would admire them. But, instead of that, the yellow old fellow cried out with
horror, and said they all three looked as if they
were turned into glass. And so, indeed, they did,
they had looked at themselves so long in the Glass

K

Mountain. Goldina had still her complexion like blanc-mange and strawberries, but it was hard like glass, and you could almost see through it; and they all seemed as if they would break to pieces if they were roughly handled. So they had to be wrapped up in cotton wool, and carried very carefully on board. And when they got home, the King and Queen cried to see their daughter, and had her put into a room padded all round with cotton wool, and gave orders that nothing hard should be brought near her, lest she should break to pieces.

And they went again to the Hermit of the Dismal Cave, to ask him what was to be done. He told them that there was no help for it now but to send her to the Woolly Land under the Earth, where all the ground and the hills were covered with wool, and there were no creatures to be seen but woolly sheep, and where they must live three years, spinning wool, and wearing nothing but woollen clothes: but they must take care, if they saw any dresses of silk or satin, not to put them on or touch them, or something very bad would happen.

So the King and Queen sent ships all over the world to find the Woolly Land under the Earth; and only one of the ships returned, the captain of which said he had found the Woolly Land under the Earth; but that it was very difficult to reach, and that the way to it was down a deep hole in the top of a mountain in a distant island, down which people must be let by ropes to get to the woolly country under ground. But the King did not care for that, as long as he could get Goldina cured.

And he sent her and the nurse and the governess off in a ship, wrapped up in cotton wool, to the island the captain had told him of. And, when they got there, they were let down the hole at the top of the mountain, and found themselves in the Woolly Land. And then they lived among the woolly sheep for nearly three years, spinning wool all day, and singing to each other, as they spun, and clothing themselves in the wool they spun, and playing with the woolly sheep, who were very kind to them. And there was one pretty little woolly sheep in particular that was very fond of Goldina. And they forgot all about their pretty looks, and all about gold, and fine dresses and vanity, and thought of nothing but spinning and singing, and being kind to the woolly sheep, and doing their duty. And, without knowing it, they got their old looks back again, and were no longer like glass. But it was so dark in that country that they could only just see each other.

One day, when the three years were nearly over,

Goldina, who always said what she thought, cried out, " I wonder how we look by this time : why should we not try to get out of this dull dark country, and see the world where the sun shines? for it is so dark here that we can hardly see each other."

But the governess scolded her, and said she was a naughty discontented little girl, and that her mind was set on vanity.

And she told the nurse to take her to bed. And the nurse scolded her again, as she did so.

But as soon as she had put her to bed, she set off herself to try to find the world where the sun was shining.

But the governess was watching for her, and caught her, and sent her to her room, and locked her in. And then she started herself to try to find the world outside, where the sun was shining. She walked a long way through the dark Woolly Country, and got very much tired ; and at last she saw an opening through the rocks, and the sun shining brightly through it. And she ran on eagerly, and looked through the opening, and saw a beautiful country full of birds and flowers and butterflies ; and there were silk dresses and neck-laces growing on the trees ; and birds and butter-flies came fluttering to her with silk dresses and jewels in their mouths, and inviting her to put

them on. As she was going to do so, she heard
a woolly sheep, who had followed her, saying "ba,
ba," in a very plaintive voice behind her, as if to
entreat her not to do so. But she took up a stone,
and threw it at the woolly sheep, like a naughty
cruel lady as she was, and took the dress and the
jewels, and put them on ; when, all at once, she
was changed into a butterfly ; and what became
of her I don't know, for nothing has been heard
of her since.

Well, the nurse, when she was left alone locked
up in her room, was very anxious to get out
again. First she tried the key-hole, but it was
too small ; and then she tried the chimney, but it
was too narrow ; and then she made a rope of her
woolly dress, and let herself down out of the
window. And it happened to her as it had done
to the governess : and another woolly sheep followed her too, and tried to lure her back by saying " ba-ba" in a plaintive voice behind her ; but
she, too, threw a stone at the poor woolly sheep,
and was changed into a butterfly ; and of her, too,
nothing has since been heard.

So poor little Goldina was left alone with the
woolly sheep in the dark woolly country. And
she felt so solitary that she thought she must set
out and try to find her nurse and governess. And,
after walking a long way, and feeling very much

tired, she came at last to the opening in the rocks, and saw the sun shining, and the birds and the butterflies, and the trees and flowers, and the beautiful silk dresses and jewels. And she was just going to take a dress which a beautiful bird offered her, when she heard the pretty little woolly sheep that was so fond of her say " ba-ba" in a very plaintive voice behind her. And, as she was a good kind girl, she ran back to him, and stroked him, and petted him, and went back with him, leaving all the fine things behind her. And she went again the next day, and it all happened as it had done the day before; and she went back with the pretty woolly sheep again, because he said " ba-ba" so piteously. But the third day, she went again; and this time the sunny country beyond the opening looked more beautiful than ever; and three most beautiful birds brought her such dazzling silks and jewels, and she thought it would be so much nicer to wear them than the plain woolly dress she had on, that she could not resist the temptation; and, though the pretty woolly sheep was crying "ba-ba" more piteously than ever, she took the fine dresses in her hand. But just as she did so, she looked back at the pretty woolly sheep, and saw a great savage bird pouncing down upon him to peck his eyes out. And she threw the silk dress and the jewels to the ground, and ran back and fought the great savage bird, and killed him. And all at once the pretty woolly sheep was changed into a beautiful prince, who told her his name was Prince Petlambko, and that he had been enchanted in the woolly country by the great savage bird, who was really a wicked enchanter, and his greatest enemy. And Goldina was hurt and bleeding with fighting the great savage bird; but Prince Petlambko cured her in a moment by breathing on her. And all at once they were at the sea-shore; and there was a magnificent ship there, with sailors magnificently dressed, who all hailed Prince Petlambko as their King. And they sailed away to Goldina's home. But, when they got there, they found the King and Queen and all the courtiers turned entirely into gold, and with no life left in them. So Goldina had another palace built of marble, and with gold in it only here and there. And the people all said that Petlambko and Goldina should be their King and Queen; and they lived happily together all their lives.

MISS BINDWEED.

THE Bindweeds are a very widely-spread family, branches of which are settled in nearly all the rural districts of England. Wherever they go they have a knack of making themselves at home, and flourishing. I am afraid, though, that their manner of life is not such as grave, long-faced people call the most creditable; for they are a regular set of vagrants, loving to rove along the hedge sides, and to climb up trees, and to trespass in farmers' fields, and seldom settling in trim cottages with gardens. Besides, they never seem able to make an independent livelihood, but prefer supporting themselves at the expense of other people, with or without their leave; and the farmers say that they are of no use at all in the parishes where they settle, and do more harm than good; and, if they could, they would generally turn them all adrift, bag and baggage. But this is more easily said than done; for, when rooted out of one place, they soon appear in another, never abashed or disconcerted. And, after all, there is a sort of wild grace about them, which takes many people's fancy, and especially that of young ladies, who are fond of visiting them in their wayside haunts, and declare that, however useless they may be, they are always good-looking, and never vulgar.

A branch of this great family was settled in a hedge which surrounded a certain corn-field in Somersetshire. Near this hedge was a high wall that bounded the garden of the great house of the parish. The family in question lived there very happily, and were very numerous. There was one member of it especially, remarkably tall and good looking, whom, by way of distinction, we will call Miss Bindweed. The Bindweeds were not usually called Mr. or Miss; but this one gave herself such airs, and affected to be such a fine lady, that the rest of the family used to call her Miss Bindweed. She had not left home yet, though most of her sisters had already wandered off in various directions to get married. Many of them had got hold of members of the Barleycorn family, who were very useful and respectable people, occupying the neighbouring field. Farmer Gruff, to whom the field belonged, was very angry at seeing this; for it was very vexing to observe the strongest and

most promising young men of the Barleycorns
get entangled with these seductive girls, who
never helped their husbands to work, but even
prevented them from doing any good, clinging
to them continually, and insisting on doing nothing but laugh and flaunt in the sunshine.
Miss Bindweed often amused herself with watching her sisters from the hedge, and with laughing at Farmer Gruff. But she had higher views
for herself; having resolved to make a grand
match. She might have been married many a
time, for she had many suitors; but they were
none of them good enough for her.

There was one very respectable young fellow
who was particularly fond of her, honest John
Thistle, who lived in the ditch beneath the hedge.
He came of a very ancient Scotch family, which
had once been of such importance that the Kings
of Scotland used to carry a picture of one of
them on their banners, when they went to battle;
and there is still always such a picture over the
Queen of England's coat of arms. Our friend,
honest John, had come sadly down in the world,
as he lived in an English ditch; but he was a
strong sturdy fellow, proud of his old descent,
and boasted that the blood of his ancestors was
still in him, for that, like them, he made any one
bleed that handled him rudely. He had, besides,

a very fine bushy head of hair of a beautiful
purple colour, and was always dressed in green.
Well, he often looked up from his ditch to Miss
Bindweed in the hedge, and requested her to
creep down and marry him; saying, that she
would be safe from harm under his protection,
far more so than with the effeminate fops, Eglantine and Woodbine, in the hedge above; and
that her pale face would contrast beautifully with
his purple hair and complexion. But she paid very
little attention to him, and preferred flirting with
Mr. Woodbine and Mr. Eglantine, who were two
elegant country exquisites, and always sweetly
scented.   As for Miss Bindweed, she never used
perfumes, and never over-dressed herself, being
remarkable for her graceful simplicity.   And this
shews that she had natural good taste.   Well,
she often amused herself with talking to these
country swells; but even they were not good
enough for her.   And I will now tell the reasons
why she had set her heart on a higher destiny.

In the first place, the bee, who flew where he
pleased, and spent a good deal of his time in the
garden at the other side of the high wall I spoke
of, often came to Miss Bindweed and told her
wonderful tales of the grand sprigs of nobility
that lived there in state; and how fine ladies and
gentlemen walked among them, and admired

them; and how the flowers themselves were often taken into the great house to enjoy themselves at the dinner-table, or to make a figure in the drawing-room and ball-room, in the society of ladies.

In the second place, one of the young ladies who lived in the great house used to ramble along the hedge where Miss Bindweed lived, and often stopped to admire her, talking poetry to her, and calling her a sweet child of Nature. She even spoke one day of taking her away with her, and wearing her in her hair at the next County ball. Miss Bindweed did not know what this meant, any more than she knew what the poetry meant which the young lady talked to her. But she had a notion that it meant something very grand and delightful; and all this, in addition to what the bee had told her, made her agog to get out of that stupid hedge into the garden of the great house, over the wall.

As for poor John Thistle, he was discarded for ever after one of the young lady's visits. I am almost ashamed to mention how rudely he had behaved. The young lady had stooped to pick a flower that grew beneath the hedge, close to John, when, in a fit of spite or jealousy, he had bitten her wrist, and actually made it bleed. After this, Miss Bindweed would not even look at him;

nor were the fascinations and scents of Mr.
Woodbine and Mr. Eglantine sufficient to detain
her from the purpose on which her heart was
now set, of getting within the garden behind the
great wall. She kept continually creeping that
way, and at last, observing a crack in the wall,
she made her way through it, and found herself,
for the first time in her life, within this magnificent garden. How dazzled she was, and how
shy she felt, at the sight of all the grandees that
lived there! They were much more splendid
than her old friends in the hedge, but hardly
looked so unconstrained and happy. They stood
in stiff rows and circles, as if they were cramped
by the manners of high life, and did not laugh
and toss themselves about in the sunshine, as her
old friends had done.

A little afraid of venturing all at once into such
high society, she crept down to a stout motherly
looking old lady, whom she observed in a retired
place, just beneath the wall. Her name was Mrs.
Cabbage-rose; and in her youth she had been a
great belle, and a leader of fashion; but she was
rather out of fashion now, and was spending her
old age in retirement. There was a pleasant sweet
atmosphere about her, that gave Miss Bindweed
confidence.

"Well," said the old lady, "so you are a

country girl, ambitious of getting into the upper circles : you had better have stayed where you were, for I can tell you from experience that fashionable life is very unsatisfactory."

Miss Bindweed then told what had induced her to try to push her fortunes, and what visions she had of the happiness in store for her in the garden.

"Foolish child," said the old lady, "you'll soon find out your mistake. Fashionable life is not now what it used to be. The good old families are getting pushed to the wall, and a race of foreign upstarts are taking their places, people whose names had not been heard of when I was young. Would you believe it? I myself am hardly noticed now, though I have the best old English blood in my veins. Take my advice, and either creep back to your hedge, or at any rate stay here with me as my companion, and do not venture further. If you go among those affected foreigners, they will only look down upon you, and perhaps you will be put to death as an in-truder. And, above all things, expect nothing good from the attentions of the grand folks from the house; I know what their pretended affection for us poor flowers means. Many a flower that has felt proud and happy at being selected for a bouquet has found out her mistake, when, having passed a hot uncomfortable evening, she has been thrown away next morning to wither and die. Sometimes even a more speedy fate awaits us. Never shall I forget what happened to a lovely and promising daughter of my own, whom one of those monsters calling themselves young ladies took a fancy to one summer morning. Proud was the look that my poor child cast back on me, as she left me resting on the creature's delicate glove; but judge of my pangs as I observed this same creature, as she walked away, deliberately pull the dear innocent thing to pieces, and scatter her remains along the gravel walk. Human beings have no hearts, my dear; and the farther you can keep away from them the better."

Notwithstanding all the good advice of kind old Mrs. Cabbage-rose, our giddy and ambitious young friend was determined to push her fortunes, and gradually crept away to the very edge of a bed where some of the most showy figures were standing. They were clothed in all kinds of brilliant colours; there were old ladies in turbans, standing stiff and upright, and young ones with gold in their hair, drooping their heads in an affected way, and gentlemen dressed in velvet coats of all the colours of the rainbow.

There was among them one towards whom Miss Bindweed felt attracted; partly because he bore

a resemblance to some of her old friends in the
hedge, of the rose family, so that she was less
afraid of him.   Still, he was much more stately
and cultivated than any of them, and she was a
little alarmed at hearing him addressed as " M.
Gloire de Dijon."   But, notwithstanding his grand
looks and grand name, she sidled towards him,
and looked up at him in the graceful way that was
natural to her.   He condescended to notice her,
being pleased with her simple white dress and
country manner; for he was a little tired of the
grandeur and affectation of his usual companions.
But when she ventured to ask him whether he
was related to the Wild-rose family whom she had
known in this country, he turned up his nose in
great disdain; and she found that no such al-
lusions to vulgar life could be allowed in that
select society.   Having a good deal of tact, she
soon adapted her manners and conversation to his
more refined taste, and they got really fond of
each other.   But matters were now going too far.
As long as she only nestled at his feet in a humble
unassuming way, the other inhabitants of the
flower-bed did not take much notice, thinking it
no harm that His Grace should amuse himself
with a country girl, and even admiring her simple
dress and manners from a lofty distance.   But
when they really seemed to be growing attached

to each other, there was a tremendous commotion in the flower-bed. All the Lady Geraniums, and the Lady Verbenas, and the Lobelias in white and blue, and the grand China-Aster family, shook their plumes, and fanned themselves, in a state of violent indignation. One tall stately young lady in particular, Miss Tiger-lily, who usually stood near M. Gloire de Dijon, and had designs upon him, shook her head so violently in her agitation that she scattered a heap of her gold ornaments on the floor. All agreed that this sort of thing must be put an end to; that their society must be kept select; that it would never do for M. Gloire de Dijon to get seriously entangled with a mere vagrant from the hedge-side. So they resolved to call the attention of the Master of the Ceremonies, M. Jardinier, to the matter, when he next came his rounds. Things were now becoming very serious for Miss Bindweed. For neither the aristocratic flowers, nor M. Jardinier himself, had any mercy or compassion towards vulgar intruders. There had been a sad instance lately of their relentless cruelty in such cases.

The Daisy family are a large and respected one, and of true English origin; they are always bright and happy and contented, and never give themselves airs, or do any one harm. A host of these pleasant people had settled on the grass-plot near

L

this aristocratic flower bed; and though they had committed no crime whatever, and really brightened the scene, M. Jardinier had sent half-a-dozen old women with hoes to destroy them all from off the face of the earth.

This relentless gentleman no sooner perceived what was up between Miss Bindweed and M. Gloire de Dijon than he set to work to separate them, taking great care not to hurt him as he did so, but paying no regard at all to Miss Bindweed's feelings. He even wounded her white skin, and dislocated one of her finger-joints by his rude treatment of her.

But happily the young lady who had taken such notice of Miss Bindweed, when living in the hedge, came by just in the nick of time; and said, "O dear! Mr. MacPherson, please don't hurt that dear little Bindweed, who is a particular favourite of mine: can't you leave her happy where she is?"

"Why you see, my lady," he replied, "this Gloire de Dijon is one of the best flowers in the garden, and we cannot let him be pulled down by mere a common weed, such as you can find in any hedge. The life of such an ordinary thing is really not worth saving."

"Still," said the young lady, "I have a great wish to save it: can't you manage it somehow?"

"Suppose then," said he, "we unite her to Sir John here, who, though of a good stock, is getting old, and is now out of fashion : perhaps he may be able to support her for a little time at least."

So our young friend was married straightway, without being asked whether she liked it or not, to old Sir John, whose full name was Sir John Hollyhock, a gouty old fellow, and rather crusty. She clung to him as affectionately as she could, as there was nothing else for her to do ; but she drooped sadly and lost her good looks, and there was not much love between them. Still, he was rather vain of his young wife; but it did not last long ; for when the first frost came he died, and left her a worn out and sickly widow.

She just managed to crawl as she could towards her old friend Mrs. Cabbage-rose, who was still as sweet as ever, and received her kindly. And there Miss Bindweed, whom we will not call Lady Hollyhock, though she had a right to the name, spent her few remaining days, under the protection of the old lady.

The Bee visited her there once more, and told her sad stories of what had happened, since she had left, in the hedge and corn-field : how the scythe of Fate had cut down all the Barleycorns, and how all the Bindweed girls who had married into that family had shared their fate : how a huge monster with great shears had come and cropped off the heads of Mr. Woodbine and Mr. Eglantine in the hedge, and of a whole host of the more ambitious Bindweeds too: and how the members of her family who had escaped were principally those who had united themselves to the Thistle family below; for that they had remained safe in their obscurity, and under the protection of those valiant sturdy fellows. Miss Bindweed uttered a feeble sigh as she thought of poor honest John Thistle, whom she had once despised so much, and thought how foolish she had been to carry her head so high. She made many other reflections which need not be put down here, since sensible readers, who can enter into the moral of this story, may all make them for themselves.

Early in the autumn she faded away and died, happy in the kind motherly care of dear Mrs. Cabbage-rose, who scattered perfumes, and shed tears as soft as dew-drops over her grave.

May all girls who have been as foolish in their youth as she was, meet with as kind a friend at last, and come to such a peaceful end!

SKIMBLE SKAMBLE AND THE BROWN MEN.

BEING THE AUTHOR'S ACCOUNT OF HIMSELF,
AND HIS OWN ADVENTURES.

IF any boys or girls that read these tales have been in the parts of England called Westmoreland and Cumberland, and have seen the lakes and mountains there, they will understand better what I am going to tell them : at least, they will be able to picture to themselves the kind of place where what I am going to tell them happened. For, as to understanding all I am going to say, they will never do that, however clever they may be. I am not sure that I understand it all myself, though I must be wonderfully clever, or I could not write such nice stories, or have seen what I am now going to tell them about.

My young friends will, perhaps, want to know who I am, and what is my name. Well, my name is Skimble Skamble, and I am a sort of wizard, I believe. At any rate, I can see things that other people cannot; I am intimately acquainted with a number of elves and fairies; and I understand the language of birds. Perhaps I was born at midnight on the 31st of February; for that would account for a great deal; perhaps I was a changeling, and really belong to fairyland. However this may be, I am a wonderful person; and I am fond of wandering among wild mountains, and in dark woods, and by lonely rivers, where I may meet with strange adventures.

One day, when I was in Cumberland, I set off alone from a place called Wonderthwaite, late in the evening; and after a time I lost myself among the mountains. At last, as it grew dark, I found myself in a gloomy ravine between very high rocks, which wound and wound about, as if there was no end to it. I heard nothing but the ravens croaking among the crags above me. They did not know that I understood them; so they talked about me freely; and what they all said was: " Look at that foolish fellow : he little knows where he is going; to-morrow morning we'll eat his eyes, and then we'll pick his bones." And then they set up a kind of hoarse, horrid, grating laugh among themselves. However, I was determined to go on, hoping to meet with some strange adventure. Indeed, it would have been of no use turning back, for I had quite lost my way, and it was getting pitch dark. So on I walked, and kept stumbling over large stones that lay in my way. After a time I fancied I heard in front of me the sound of somebody whistling, and sometimes singing at the pitch of his voice in harsh shrill tones. But it was too dark for me to see anyone. The sound seemed to go on as I went on : indeed, the person who uttered them seemed to be travelling very fast; for I had much difficulty in keeping within hearing of his voice. At last the moon appeared, and I perceived about a hundred yards in front of me a most extraordinary figure. It was that of a man about four feet high, dressed in brown, who went springing from rock to rock with wonderful activity, singing or whistling all the time. I shouted after him ; but he paid no attention to me. So, being determined to get at him, I ran forward as fast as I could, and, when I had got near enough, threw a large stone at him, and hit him on the head. He uttered a tremendous yell, and turned round, roaring at me full of fury. His face was as brown as earth, and looked a hundred years old. But he must have been wonderfully strong; for he heaved from the ground a huge stone, far bigger than I could have lifted, raising it above his head

in his long arms as if he meant to throw it at me.
And so he did: but I slipped out of the way. He
then rushed at me with a loud roar, seized me in
his long skinny arms, and would have dashed me
against the rocks in a moment, if—

I told you before that I was a wonderful person.
If I had not been so, I should not now have been
alive to tell this wonderful tale. But I had long
heard of the brown men of the moors and mountains, though I had never met with one before,
and a very wise old woman had once told me of a
charm by means of which they might be appeased
when angry. The charm was this: to put one's
mouth close to the brown man's ear, and say,
"Munko tiggle snobart tolwol dixy crambo." I
had great difficulty in managing this: for, as I
told you, he had got me tight and lifted up in his
skinny arms. But by wriggling myself with a
tremendous effort, I succeeded. All at once he
put me down, and looked at me with wondering
eyes. Of course you want to know what these
words meant, and why they had such an effect
upon him. Don't be too curious, my dears.
Haven't you often been told that young people
ought not be curious? In order to teach you this
lesson, which you are too apt to forget, I don't
intend to tell you the meaning of these strange
words. All you need know is that they made the

little man quite kind and civil; and, if you ever
meet with a brown man of the moors and mountains, try for yourselves if they do not answer.

I told you the little man put me down, and grew
quite kind and civil. He was more than civil:
he seemed to regard me as his master, and asked
what he could do to serve me. Finding him in
this humour, I thought it best to make the most
of it; so I put on a commanding air, called him a
little brown cur, and ordered him to make amends
for his late rudeness by shewing me a place to
lodge in for the night, and by answering all the
questions I might ask him, and telling no lies.
He promised to do so, and trudged on before me
still further up the ravine, till he came to a small
hole beneath a rock, where he stopped, and
whistled three times. Presently a torch appeared
at the mouth of the hole, into which he crept,
guided by the light, bidding me follow him. I
did so, and, after creeping for a long time on
hands and knees after the light that went before
us, we came at last to a magnificent hall, lighted
with torches, in which immense heaps of gold and
of diamonds were piled on the floor. Round a
table in the middle of the hall sat six other little
brown men at supper, each of them looking at
least a hundred years old.

They jumped up on seeing me, and rushed at

me as if to strangle me. But, on my companion
saying some words to them that I did not understand, they became civil and obsequious, just as
he had done after I had whispered in his ear those
strange words, of which you want so much to
know the meaning, "Munko tiggle snobart tolwol
dixy crambo." They all asked me what they
could do to serve me. "Brown dogs," I said,
"give me supper first; and then answer all my
questions, and tell no lies." They all waited on
me as I supped. It was very queer stuff that they
gave me to eat; but, as I was hungry, I thought
it best not to ask what it was. When I had done,
I began to question them, and the following conversation passed between us :— ↙

I. Who are you, and what is your employ-
ment?

THEY. My lord, you are pleased to affect igno-
rance; but you know that we are the remnant of
the Brown Men of the Moors and Mountains, who
formerly lived all over England and Scotland,
but now live only in this cave.

I. Never mind what I know, or what I don't
know, but answer me truly. How has it come
to pass that from being a great nation, you are
now reduced to such small numbers?

THEY. The world has changed during the last
five hundred years, and especially in the last

hundred. Men have made roads and built houses in our old haunts, and driven us away. And when driven away and frightened, most of us die. Besides, men have written such a lot of books, and grown so clever, that they don't believe in us; and that breaks our hearts, and kills us. But nothing has done us so much harm as those awful iron roads, and fiery monsters drawing trains of carriages, which nowadays go screaming all about the country. The very sound of them has often frightened a whole tribe of us to death. Here we manage to live, because men seldom come here; and if any stray wanderer does come here, we kill him, and the ravens eat his eyes and pick his bones. We would have killed you if you had not proved yourself to be lord of the mines of gold and diamonds.

I. How do you employ yourselves?

THEY. By day we dig in the mountains for gold and diamonds; and by night we feast in our cave, or dance on the brown moors; but it is our greatest delight to kill any man that we can catch alone in these solitudes, and watch the ravens eat his eyes, and pick his bones.

I. A very creditable amusement! and it shows you to be good fellows. But you were more amiable in old times, before persecution and fear made you spiteful. But now I want to know

more, and to see more, for this hall is not the
only place you have got to show me. Show me
all your treasures, and disclose all your secrets.

THEY. O, my lord, you have seen all that is
worth seeing. Help yourself to all this gold, and
these diamonds, and be satisfied. We have indeed one little cave more, but there are no treasures in it; and it is not fit for the inspection of
a great lord like you.

I. Brown dogs, and slaves, dare not to trifle
with me! I would see all. " Munko tiggle
snobart tolwol dixy crambo."

On hearing these terrible words, which I uttered in a loud, gruff voice, they all seemed
afraid, and, after whispering awhile to each other,
led me to the farthest corner of the cave, and,
rolling away a stone, showed me a long, narrow,
dark passage, leading upwards through the rocks.
I made a sign to one of them to lead the way,
and followed him through the passage, which
seemed interminable, but ended at last in a small
room, dimly lighted by means of a crack in the
roof, through which the moon was shining.
When I had been there long enough to see what
was in it, I perceived a beautiful little girl, with
long golden hair, which she was wreathing with
a string of diamonds, using a small pool of clear
water as a looking-glass. She was beautifully

but strangely dressed, and seemed quite startled at the sight of me. I saw at once that she was a real human being, and not one of the tribe of the brown men ; and, conjecturing that she was some poor child whom they had caught and were keeping prisoner, I exclaimed in a commanding voice, " This, then, is the treasure that was not worth my seeing, and that you were trying to hide from me, deceitful slaves ! Know ye not that this is the Princess of the Golden Locks, who is destined to be my Queen ? Release her at once, or you will feel my vengeance." They seemed much distressed at hearing this command, and before obeying me whispered to each other ; after which one of them came to me, and said, in a timid voice, " Snaro snipple snopash," and then waited for an answer. My knowledge did not enable me to make the reply they expected; and, on their repeating the words several times, and perceiving me quite at a loss, they gradually threw off their respectful manner, and became loud and insolent. They told me I was an impostor ; that I had tried to pass myself off as the lord of the mines of gold and diamonds, but that I was nothing of the kind; since, if I were, I should know how to reply. This was true enough ; but the thought of its being true did not tend to make me comfortable. After insulting and beating me for some time, they took counsel together, and then left me for the present in the cave with this maiden; and I heard their hideous croaking laughter as they retired along the passage.

It was some comfort to me that they had not killed me on the spot, though I feared that their intention was to punish me the more terribly by and by. However, I hoped to escape them after all by the aid of my wonderful cleverness, and I at once turned round to talk to the golden-haired girl.

After recovering from her first alarm, she was very affable, and delighted to talk once more with a being of her own race. She told me that she was the daughter of a shepherd in one of the valleys of the country; that, having gone for a treat with her father on the mountains one day, just one hundred years ago, she had got into her present trouble by being disobedient: for that he had strictly charged her to keep near where he left her, as he went to seek a stray sheep, and by no means to venture near a gully, or ravine, which he pointed out to her at a distance; but that, as soon as he was out of sight, curiosity had got the better of obedience, and she had gone into this gully, where a little brown man had surprised her, and carried her off to this cave, where she had been ever since. From this sad history my young readers may learn that disobedience ——. But I will go on with my story for fear of being prosy. I said I could not understand how all this could have happened a hundred years ago, since she did not look more than fourteen years old. She said that among the brown men people never grew any older than they were, and that the brown men themselves had never looked any younger than they did now, and would never look any older. I then asked her how she had spent her time all these hundred years. She said that she had been the brown men's housekeeper; that, when they were out on the moors, she had to creep through the long dark passage, and make their hall ready for them, and prepare their supper, and then creep back to her own little cave, and dress herself as grand as possible; and that, on hearing their whistle, she had to creep again to their hall and entertain them after their supper by dancing and singing to them. She added that, though they were a savage set of monsters, they were fond of her, and generally very kind to her, and particularly liked to see her grandly dressed, and adorned with gold and diamonds.

"But where," said I, " do all these fine dresses come from?"

She replied that the brown men brought them

to her, being wonderfully clever in all kinds of workmanship; the gold and diamonds they dug from the bowels of the earth, and made them into necklaces, ear-rings, and other ornaments; the dresses they spun and wove, and made up out of the stalks of ferns, or the wool and fur of animals; and the skins of various creatures supplied them with materials for her boots and white gloves.

The little vain thing seemed really quite happy in talking of all this finery, and showing me the various articles of dress that were stowed away in her cave, saying, as she did so, that it was not such a bad life after all, and that, though the brown men were not handsome, at any rate they knew what was. I was a little shocked that she took this view of things, and was on the point of giving her a lecture on the vanity of girls, and on their thinking more of fine clothes than of things of more importance. But I was afraid of boring her, as I always am of boring any young people. I almost wish, though, that I had said what I thought of saying, as reading it might have done other girls good, as well as the girl I was then talking to. However, I said nothing to her about it, but admired all her fine things, which she put on, one after another, to please me. As she was doing so, I thought I heard a cawing and croaking through the crack which I told you let light into the cave through the roof; and I asked her what that noise was. She told me that it came from a raven's nest, which was built above, and that the tiresome birds often disturbed her by their foolish conversation, which she did not understand. I begged her to be silent, if she possibly could, for a few minutes at least; for she had talked incessantly since we had been left together, being rather a chatterbox, like some other little girls. She complied, though rather sulkily, and went to look at herself in the pool of water. I then listened to what the ravens were talking about, and heard one say to another, " I heard voices in the cave below. Whom has Golden-hair got to talk to her? For it was not the voice of one of the brown men."

" Don't you know?" replied the other. " It's that foolish fellow Skimble Skamble, who has got himself into a nice scrape. We shall still have the pleasure of eating his eyes and picking his bones."

" O yes, I know," said a third; " he thought to impose upon the brown men; but he only knew half his business. He had learnt to say, ' Munko tiggle snobart tolwol dixy crambo;' but when they asked him, ' Snaro snipple snopash,' he did not know what to reply."

M

"I know what he ought to have done," said a fourth; "he ought to have snapped his right hand finger, and scratched his left ear, and said, 'Snogwollodrum.' But he'll never know that; and to-morrow we will eat his eyes, and pick his bones." After this all the ravens laughed hoarsely and horribly together, and then flew away.

I now told the young lady that she might talk again, which she was ready enough to do. As soon as I could get a word of my own in, I explained to her that, by the help of what I had heard the ravens say, I hoped to be able to rescue her presently from her awful bondage. At first she clapped her little hands for joy, but presently asked in a hesitating way whether she could take her dresses and jewels away with her.

"Foolish girl," said I, "to think of such trifles when you have the prospect of getting again among your fellow-creatures, out of the clutches of these atrocious dwarfs!"

"I am not so foolish as you think," she replied archly, "for I remember what it was to be meanly dressed, when I lived in my father's hut; and I am sure it is much nicer to be dressed well. Besides, when I go out into the world, all my relations and friends will have been dead long ago,

so that there will be nobody to take care of me;
and my success in life may depend on my being
able to make a good appearance."

There was nothing to be said against this argu-
ment, though I did not quite like it from the lips
of so young a girl; but I concluded that living
so long with the brown men had made her
wideawake beyond her apparent years; which
was indeed the case, as I afterwards found.

Scarcely had we done speaking, when the
dwarfs returned, snorting and screaming after
their supper and wine. I stood to receive them
on a raised ledge at the remote end of the cave,
having the girl by my side, and my arm round
her waist; the sight of which made them still
more furious. I exclaimed, at the top of my voice,
"Munko tiggle snobart tolwol dixy crambo."
They replied by shaking their fists, and waving
their arms, and making hideous faces expressive
of rage, and screaming out all together, " Snaro
snipple snopash!" I then snapped my right
hand fingers, and scratched my left ear; at which
they were silent, and watched me attentively.
Taking advantage of the silence, I said slowly
and majestically, " Snogwollodrum!" The effect
was instantaneous. They fell on their knees before me, begging pardon, and again asked what
they could do to serve me.

" Rebellious dogs," I exclaimed, " first, collect, and remove into the great hall, all the dresses and trinkets belonging to this young lady, my Queen; pack them in three chests that three of you can carry on your shoulders, fill another chest with diamonds, and then await our further orders."

They obeyed, though with evident reluctance, the young lady in the meantime ordering them about pretty sharply, and taking care that they left none of the best things behind, as the sly fellows seemed inclined to do.

When all was packed, and we were all assembled in the large hall, I commanded them to take up the chests, and convey them and us to a cave which I named, from which I knew the road to the inhabited part of the country. They did so, it being still dark, though they seemed much alarmed at going so far from their usual haunts. In this cave they left the chests; and then I let them go.

The young lady, who was delighted with the adventure, and kept clapping her little hands and laughing loudly, was anxious to beat them all round with an ash stick, before they went off, in order, she said, to pay off old scores: but this I would not allow. As soon as I dismissed them, they ran off over the rocks with incredible swiftness ; and I have never seen them since.

As soon as it was light, I proceeded to the nearest village, and had the chests removed, with which I and the girl went to London by the next train. On arriving there, I was at a loss what to do with the poor girl, who I feared would be so friendless in the world. But she soon relieved me from my anxiety. For next day she appeared before me at lunch time (having gone out alone early in the morning), dressed in the height of the modern fashion. She told me that she had been to a milliner's, in order to equip herself decently for modern life, and that she was now going to take leave of me, having resolved to go to Paris, and there pass herself off as an Eastern Princess, and make her fortune. She then gave me a small bag of gold, and a few magnificent diamonds, as my reward, and parted from me with much affection, but with a condescending air. I have never seen her since: but I have heard of a beautiful Eastern Princess, believed to be immensely rich, having arrived in Paris, and of the report that she was going to be married to some great French lord.

As for me, I have lived since that time as I did

before; wandering among wild mountains, and in dark woods, and by lonely rivers, seeking adventures, and learning tales, which I tell for the amusement and moral improvement of young people, of whom I am so fond.

Here you have a few of them, which I hope you have liked, my little friends. My own children, for whose amusement I wrote them, say they like them very much; and this encourages me to hope that others will like them too. If you don't care about them, I fear it is because they are stupid: for I cannot think that any of you are such little prigs as to fancy yourselves too clever to care for fairy tales at all. With children like that, if there are any such, I really have no patience. As for you, Papas and Mamas, Uncles and Aunts, I cannot expect you (people are so wise now-a-days) to care much for tales like these. Still, for the sake of your children, nephews, and nieces, I hope you will view them with a favourable eye. At any rate pray don't object to them because they are not true, or because you don't see the moral of them. Perhaps there is both truth and moral enough to be found in them if you have wit enough to discover it. And it is a bad thing for children to be too constantly preached at. However this may be, if these tales have caused any of my little friends to open their eyes in wonder, or to enjoy a merry laugh, it is enough for their affectionate friend,

SKIMBLE SKAMBLE.